Maiden in Manhattan

A Timeless Love Series (Book 1)

(Originally published as Lost in Time I)

Abbie Zanders

This is a work of fiction. Similarities to real people, places, or events are entirely coincidental.

First edition (Lost in Time I). September, 2014.

Second edition (Maiden in Manhattan). January, 2016

Copyright © 2014, 2015, 2016 Abbie Zanders.

Written by Abbie Zanders.

All rights reserved.

ISBN: 1523308664
ISBN-13: 978-1523308668

Acknowledgements

Special thanks to:

… Carol Tietsworth for her mad proofreading skills; if you find an error, I made it *after* she looked at it.

… Cindy, Susie, and Aubrey for their infinite patience and willingness to put up with me.

… Heather Black | Studio 410 Designs, for her beautiful, one-of-a-kind custom photos and cover design. (Background image: pixabay.com)

… and to all of *you* for selecting this book – you didn't have to, but you did. Thanks ☺

Before You Begin

Please note that due to strong language and some steamy romantic interludes, this book is intended for mature (18+) readers. If this is not you, then

1. Shame on you.
2. Give this book to your mother (or other mature adult) and let *them* enjoy it.

Prologue

Isobeille Aislinn McKenna was a survivor, but in a quiet, unassuming way. She had not a cruel bone in her body, and was more likely to kindly move a bug out of harm's way than to crush it beneath her tiny feet. She was gentle of soul, mild of manner, delicate of form, and had the serene and calming beauty of an angel.

If her prayers had gone unanswered, she would have found a way to endure in that peaceful, quiet way of hers.

She would have made the best of her situation.

She would have married the knight with nary another complaint.

She would have striven to be a kind and dutiful wife, to serve her husband in all the ways the Lord intended.

She would have allowed all of her fanciful dreams of adventure and freedom and true love to fall, unrealized and unrecognized, by the wayside as she went on.

But as it turned out, she didn't have to.

Chapter 1

Isobeille barely had time to bring her hands up to cover her eyes. The beast was massive, bigger than any dragon, with scales so smooth it was impossible to tell where one left off and another began.

And its eyes! Great glowing orbs as bright as the midday sun flashed before her, instantly blinding her while letting out a deafening roar. The sound was quite unlike anything she had ever heard before; it reverberated through her entire body and made her teeth tremble right along with the rest of her.

The scream didn't even have a chance to wrench its way from her throat before she felt a bone-jarring force lifting her from her feet. After only a moment or two of weightlessness, her body landed hard on an unforgiving surface and a crushing weight expelled all of the breath from her lungs.

"Jesus Christ, lady! You got a death wish or something?"

It took a moment for the words to penetrate the

haze of terror, but when they did, Isobeille realized the heaviness across her torso was warm and moving. While substantial, it was much smaller than the silvery beast that had tried to take her in its great and powerful maws. This made sense, now that her wits were beginning to return to her; the attack had come from the side, not from the front as expected.

She tried desperately to draw breath, even as her mind began to sort through the happenings of the last several moments. When it did, an odd scent entered with it. Decidedly male, though so very different from any of the scents she had come to associate with men. It was spicy and fresh, musky but not unwashed.

Her heavy lids lifted slowly to reveal the visage of a man only inches from her face. Tousled brown hair fell haphazardly over hypnotically beautiful eyes. They were warm, a shade of clear, dark brown with exceptionally long lashes. Isobeille could not help but think that they were the eyes of a kind man, despite the fact that they now held a hint of indignant fury.

"Well?" the man said impatiently, his breath both warm and yet cool over her skin.

The substantial form continued to press upon her breast, rendering her incapable of uttering anything more than a soft, decidedly feminine murmur. As quiet as it was, it was sufficient to convey her discomfort. With a deep grunt of his own, the stranger pushed away and rolled to the side. Isobeille took the opportunity to expand her lungs, wincing at the sharp stab of resulting pain.

With some effort, she leveraged herself into a sitting position. When her hand stung in protest, she noticed that it was scraped and bleeding, but nothing worrisome. Much more interesting was the strange, semi-smooth, gray pathway beneath it. Intrigued, she scraped at it with her fingernail. 'Twas unlike anything she had seen before.

"Hey. She okay?" Another voice spoke in close proximity. As the ringing between her ears began to subside, Isobeille realized she was surrounded by a small crowd of people. It consisted of both males and females by the looks of it, though it was hard to tell which was which in some cases because of the strange garments they wore.

Even more bizarre than the motley gathering, the skies above them were dark. That suggested a time far beyond the gloaming, yet she could see each of their faces clearly and not one carried a torch.

"Maybe she's in shock," said another voice, drawing Isobeille's eyes downward again. This one was high-pitched and carried a slight nasal twang, like a woman's, but the one who spoke didn't look like any female Isobeille had ever seen. She wore tight leggings like a man, and skinny stilts beneath her feet. Her hair was shorn close, and of a vivid color that reminded Isobeille of a robin's egg. Eyes heavily outlined in dark coal suddenly filled Isobeille's field of vision as her nostrils were assaulted with a pungent perfume.

"Hey, honey. Do you know where you are?"

Cold fear swiftly gripped Isobeille's heart as she looked around at these strange people in their strange dress. At the lights glowing above her. *Colored lights with no visible flame.* At the stream of gleaming metallic demons in all colors of the rainbow rushing only a short distance from where she sat, *moving without the draw of horses*. Tears filled her eyes as she shook her head. This was like no place she had ever seen.

Suddenly that man's face was before her again – the one with the warm brown eyes. Some of his rage seemed to have faded, but he still looked far from pleased.

"How many fingers am I holding up?" he asked, his voice slightly rough and lightly scented with peppermint. He spoke with an accent she could not place. English, she thought, though different than the kind she was used to. Without thinking, she answered him in her native language, the words rolling naturally off her tongue.

The man muttered something just beneath his breath. She had displeased him again; she didn't have to understand all the words to know that.

"Maybe she doesn't speak English," someone suggested, confirming her initial suspicions. "What language is that, anyway?"

Was she in England, then? She had been there once, when she was but a girlchild, but it did not look anything like this. And even in England surely they would have recognized her native Gaelic. Hated her for it, perhaps, but recognized it all the same.

Attempting to gain purchase over her fear, she focused on his hands, fascinated by them. They were nice hands, large and strong, with long fingers and the calluses of one who earned an honest living. Her arm rose up, pressing her much smaller hand against his. His eyes widened slightly at the odd pulse where they touched.

"Hey man, I think she likes you," somebody chuckled.

"She should. He saved her life. Did you see that crazy bitch, standing in front of the cross-town bus like that?"

"Yeah, you're a fucking hero, man."

Isobeille blinked. Several of the words were unfamiliar. She had no idea what a *cross-town bus* was. But she did understand that this man had somehow saved her from the silvery beast.

"*Tapadh liebh*," she said, bowing her head. "Thank you," she repeated in heavily accented English. His eyes softened for just a moment before hardening again.

* * *

This was the last thing he needed, Nick thought, looking down into a pair of the biggest green eyes he had ever seen. It was a color he'd never seen in a pair of human eyes before, the exact shade of a tropical sea. Or at least what he thought was the color of a tropical sea. Since the only references he had were from movies and television, he could be wrong.

There was no denying the clarity, nor the way they seemed to flash and sparkle like finely cut gems. Surely it was a trick of the light.

Or something.

Adrenaline was still coursing through his veins at incredible speed; it was a natural, instinctive reaction brought on by the sight of a woman about to be flattened by a bus and the sudden need to prevent said flattening from occurring.

Of course, his body also seemed to be experiencing another natural, instinctive reaction, although this one had nothing to do with imminent physical peril and everything to do with the soft, feminine body that had cushioned his fall.

Nick took a deep breath, hoping to stem both. He was already running late; that last call out to the accident just outside the tunnel had taken him well past the end of his shift, but there were things more important than punching a clock. Gloria was going to be really pissed if he messed up again. If he had one ounce of common sense, he would have just kept his head down like everyone else and kept walking.

Except he couldn't. Try as he might, there was still something deep down inside of him that made him the world's biggest sucker at every available opportunity.

Now that he had done his good deed for the day, it was time to move on.

"You're welcome," he said gruffly.

Nick pushed himself to his feet and held his hand out to her. She looked at it for a moment, then at him, before tentatively putting her hand in his. He felt the same rush he'd felt earlier, when she'd pressed her palm to his, but he ignored it. Had to be adrenaline or endorphins, or some shit like that.

Didn't matter. She didn't seem to be hurt badly, just a little scraped and stunned. And he needed to be hauling ass.

"Where are you going? Can I call you a cab?" he asked impatiently as he tugged, lifting her to her feet with little effort. The small crowd around them dispersed, the momentary drama already just a brief sound bite in their memories. He extracted a monogrammed handkerchief from his pocket – a Christmas gift from his mother – and pressed it to her bleeding hand before wiping his own hastily on his jeans.

A pretty pink blush painted her cheeks as she smoothed down her dress with her other hand. He hardened himself against that, too, taking notice of her unusual outfit for the first time: a long skirt that brushed the pavement, tight-fitted bodice that teased him with the hint of lush breasts, and full sleeves that gathered tightly around the wrist. The covering she'd worn over her hair now lay in the middle of the busy street, freeing her long, dark red tresses to spill well past her hips in voluminous waves. She looked like some sort of medieval peasant girl. As costumes went, he had to admit, it was a good one.

His impatience grew as she worried her bottom lip, her gaze looking around as if she had no clue where she was.

"What is this place?" she asked, her voice small, her words heavily accented.

"You're kidding, right?" he said in disbelief. Those eyes, those big, green eyes, looked at him. *Who had eyes like that?*

"Nay."

Nay? What kind of answer was that? If he didn't know for a fact that he'd cushioned her head with his now-throbbing arm he would have thought she'd whacked it good.

"What is your name?" Nick shifted his weight from one foot to the other as he reached down into his front pocket for a couple of bills. He didn't have time for this, but his innate chivalry wouldn't allow him to just tackle and run.

Pretty, rose-colored lips curved slightly in a tentative smile. "Isobeille."

The effect was startling; it hit him somewhere in the dead center of his chest and shot right down to his balls, which were still protesting the absence of all that lush softness against the length of him. He quite forcefully (and thankfully silently) told them to shut the fuck up.

"Isobeille," he repeated, but it didn't sound the same as when she said it. With her accent, the name had rolled off her tongue like music.

Nick shook himself. What the hell was he thinking? Gloria was expecting dinner, wine, and roses. Things hadn't been going especially well with her lately, not since he screwed up and asked her to travel back with him to his family's house for Thanksgiving. This might be his last chance. He needed to wrap this up and get home, shower, and shave. His cock pulsed, reminding him that maybe he should pick up a couple of extra condoms on the way...

But first he had to get this woman somewhere safe so his conscience would be clear. Maybe she had family nearby.

"Isobeille what?"

Instead of answering, she pressed her lips together and shook her head slightly. Nick frowned. He looked down at his watch, his scowl deepening when he saw the time.

"Fine. You don't want to tell me, no skin off my nose. Here's forty bucks. That should cover a cab anywhere in the city. Any farther than that and you're out of luck, sweetheart."

She looked at the two bills he held out to her as

if she had never seen anything like them. When she made no move to take them, he shoved them into her hand and closed her fingers around them.

"Damn it, I'm really late. You're going to be alright, yeah?"

Against his will, his eyes were drawn to her lips again where she was nibbling the lower one. It was just slightly plumper than the one above it, made shiny and slightly darker by her worrying.

"Aye," she finally nodded, drawing herself up to her full height so that her gaze was leveled somewhere around his chest.

Nick forced himself to take a step back so he could look into her face rather than at the top of her head. He'd known she was small - she'd felt like nothing when he'd tackled her out of the path of the bus – but he had chalked most of that impression up to the adrenaline rush and the subsequent feel of feminine softness beneath him. Now he realized that she really was slight. He was no giant by any means. A respectable six-two, two-twenty or thereabouts. Which put her around... five-two? *Maybe*.

"Right. Take care, then."

He remained fixed in place, knowing he should move, yet he couldn't quite bring himself to do so. After several moments, she raised her chin – a show of courage if he ever saw one – and nodded again. Fisting her small hands in her skirts, she lifted them up and turned away from him.

Nick watched her make her way slowly against the rush of people coming the other way, her gait jerky and unsure, until she disappeared around the corner. It was only after she was no longer in his sights that his brain registered what his eyes had seen: she'd been barefoot.

Sooooo not his problem.

He forced himself to turn away and head back towards his place, rubbing his palm absently against his jeans, his skin still tingling from where he'd touched her like some kind of residual static shock, his cock suddenly aching like a bitch – when had *that* happened? – and the haunting green eyes of a young woman way out of her element flashing in his mind no matter how many neon signs he looked at trying to get rid of them.

He made it all of two blocks before turning around.

"Fuck," he cursed softly, jogging after her.

Chapter 2

Isobeille was at a loss, unsure what to do. It was hard to know where you were going when you had no idea where you were. When she had closed her eyes and made that fervent prayer, she really had not expected it to be granted quite so suddenly. Perhaps she should have thought it out a bit more carefully before just blurting it out like that, but it was her innermost heart that had done the talking, not her head.

It would have been nice to have landed somewhere a wee less populated, mayhap a place not quite so unfamiliar or seemingly wrought with danger, but it was a little late to think of those things now. For one brief moment she panicked, tempted to withdraw her impulsive but heartfelt wish; for never in her wildest imagination could she have foreseen a place like *this*.

So many people, all moving as though they had an urgent purpose, wearing the most outlandish clothing. Tall structures, seemingly built of stone but not, extending up into the sky all around her. So much noise, so many colors, so much everything. Her senses were being assaulted on all levels at once, addling her mind and her ability to think clearly. Where were the trees? The grass? Was there nothing familiar in this strange new place?

Her steps slowed until she stopped altogether. Isobeille turned around in a circle, looking for a way out of the pulsing throng currently swarming around her and casting curious looks her way. Surely there must be some place where she could take a few moments to catch her breath and *think*; a glen or a copse, perhaps. But where?

It was unfortunate that her bonnie rescuer had fled. For a few hopeful moments, she was certain he had felt the same instant connection she had flare to life when his much larger hand encompassed her smaller one. A strange tingling had worked its way up her arm from the point of contact, causing her breath to hitch and an odd fluttering sensation to appear in her chest.

But the flash in his eyes had dimmed all too quickly, leading her to believe that it had been nothing more than wishful thinking on her part. Then he had asked her surname, no doubt with the intent of returning her to her sire. Given her current situation that was unlikely, but Isobeille refused to take any chances. Logic suggested that if she had been brought here to this strange new world, then she could also be returned to hers as well.

Even frightened and alone, she knew which she preferred: freedom.

And perhaps his hasty departure was for the best. Despite the obvious differences in language and culture, Isobeille had recognized the look of desperation in his eyes, his need to flee apparent.

So he hadn't felt the same tingle of awareness, that sense of rightness that she had; it was what it was. Sulking over it would change nothing, and she had enough to be getting on with.

Swallowing her disappointment, Isobeille drew upon her courage. She had been given a rare gift, and she would do well not to squander it.

* * *

Nick didn't see her at first. He paused around the corner from where he'd last seen her, looking left and right, certain that she could not have gotten very far. He was right. Barely fifty feet ahead, he caught a momentary flash of dark red. Of course, all he really had to do was watch the people in the immediate vicinity, turning around to look curiously upon the odd young woman so out of place in a city of freaks.

He slowed his pace as he came up behind her, unwilling to startle her. Her expression was clearly visible, reflected in the huge panes of glass of the display window beside her. *Christ*. Had anyone ever looked so lost?

"Hey," he said. She turned at the sound of his voice. Nick refused to acknowledge the brightening in her eyes even as he rubbed absently at his chest. The relief and hope he saw in her face had nothing to do with him, really. He was just the dumbass stupid enough not to walk away.

She shivered, her arms wrapped around her midsection in a hug that made the swell of her breasts rise up above those thin leather laces holding her top together. It took a moment for him to process that, given the flare of lust that particular picture inspired.

"Are you cold?" he heard himself asking.

Brilliant. Of course she was cold. Anyone in a dress and bare feet would be at a temperature of thirty-seven degrees. The constant breeze tunneling through the skyscrapers didn't do much for the wind chill, either.

In a chivalrous move, Nick took off his leather jacket and draped it over her shoulders. He, at least, had a thermal beneath his SUNY hoodie, and fingerless gloves. Oh yeah. And *boots*.

She tilted her head and inhaled along the collar, her eyes shuttering down half-way as if she found the scent pleasing.

Ah, hell. He didn't need this right now, not when he and Gloria hadn't hooked up for weeks, a situation he was hoping to remedy very soon. He looked left, then right, searching for the hidden camera or some douchebag recording on his iPhone. Maybe he was being punked.

No cameras. Lots of douchebags. But no one

seemed unusually fixated on them or was pointing anything at them that he could see. She was getting lots of looks, though. Mostly leers. And why not? She was gorgeous - small, but built like the St. Paulie Girl. All she needed was a couple of tankards in each hand and she'd be a ringer for the poster that had adorned his college roommate's wall through their junior and senior years.

Right. Not helping.

"Okay, so look. I don't know what your deal is, but I think it's safe to say we need to get you someplace warm and safe." She blinked, looked up at him with those hypnotic green eyes, and smiled.

What the hell? He rubbed at his chest again. It felt like someone had just lit a charge in there or something. It was kind of like the ache in his groin, just suddenly there and not easily ignored.

"Isobeille, right?" he said, feeling like some punk teen with a hard-on. "I'm Nick. Nick Peterson."

"Nick Peterson," she repeated with a gentle smile, placing a breathy emphasis on the hard "k" sound at the end that he didn't think he could recreate if he tried.

"Uh, are you lost?"

A dark cloud passed over her features. "Aye," she admitted. "It appears that I am at that."

Her voice was as beautiful as the rest of her, so soft and soothing. When combined with her accent – which he now guessed to be either an Irish or

Scottish brogue – it sounded like music to his ears.

"Do you know anyone in the city? Have a place to go?"

Those delicate shoulders slumped slightly before straightening again. "Alas, I doona."

Sympathy warred with anger. He felt bad for her, he really did, but how moronic was it to come to a big city like this without having a clue?

Anger edged ahead of the sympathy. "So, what – you were just planning on winging it? Maybe finding a nice cozy spot behind a dumpster till something came along?"

The moment the words were out of his mouth he felt like a dick. She was looking at him with those big, green puppy eyes and it actually *hurt*. He rubbed at his chest again, harder this time, in an attempt to relieve the ache.

"Christ, stop looking at me like that, will you?"

Isobeille obediently dropped her eyes. He didn't think it was possible, but that made him feel even worse. He ran a hand through his hair, mussing it in the process. Either she was one hell of an actress – which she very well might be, given the get-up, or she was, as his mother would say, right off the boat.

If it was the latter, as he was beginning to suspect, she wasn't going to last one night in the city. What the hell had she been thinking?

Nick exhaled heavily. He really should think about getting the word "SUCKER" tattooed right across his forehead, but he couldn't help it if he had a conscience the size of Mount Rushmore. He blamed his mother; for as long as he could remember she was forever dragging him and his siblings along with her to soup kitchens and food drives, retirement homes and on Meals on Wheels deliveries.

"Right. So you're new in town, you don't know anybody, and you have nowhere to go. Does that about cover it?"

Isobeille nodded, but kept her eyes averted.

Nick put his finger under her chin and coaxed her face upward so he could see her eyes. "Hey, look. I'm sorry. I'm just running a little late, and my girlfriend's going to be really pissed if I don't – ah, shit." He cursed as his cell phone began to ring from his leather jacket.

Ignoring Isobeille's curious looks, he reached into the pocket and extracted the phone.

"Hey baby... yeah, of course, just running a little late but ... yeah... uh-huh... Sure, sure I understand... No, I know, if I'd been on time... right... okay... no, tomorrow's great... Talk to you then."

He snapped the lid closed and blew out a breath. Suddenly there was a butterfly-light touch on his arm.

"Nick? Is your baby okay?"

"What? I don't have a baby." As he spoke, his mind was rewinding, trying to figure out what he might have said or done to give her the impression he had a kid.

"Oh – no, that was my girlfriend."

"Your girl-friend is an infant?" she asked, her brow furrowed in obvious confusion. It was kind of adorable, really.

"No, of course not. Her name is Gloria. *Baby* is kind of my nickname for her."

She nodded, her expression clearing as understanding dawned. "Ah. It is a term of endearment. Like *sweetling*," she said.

"Sweetling, huh?" he asked, half of his mouth turning up in a grin, despite his irritation. "I like that."

Isobeille blushed, a pretty, light pink that highlighted her green eyes and dark red hair.

"Well," he said, "fortunately for you, it looks like my calendar just freed up for tonight. What do you say we grab something to eat and try to figure out just what we're going to do with you?"

Her smile was back, and strangely enough, he didn't feel quite as disappointed about having to postpone his date with Gloria as he might have. Nick told himself it was only because nothing remotely interesting had happened to him for a while, nothing more. It didn't get much more interesting than tackling a sexy Scottish peasant girl and taking her back to his place.

Nick hesitated as he realized that was what he was planning to do. Shouldn't he take her to a police station or a hospital or a shelter or something? That would probably be better. They would know what to do with her, and be better equipped to handle this kind of thing, surely. They dealt with this kind of thing all the time.

Except... she was gazing up at him with those pretty green eyes, looking way too innocent to be left in any of those places. And maybe, just maybe, he wasn't ready to turn her loose just yet.

In an old-fashioned gesture, Nick held out his arm. Isobeille accepted, her eyelashes fluttering slightly as she did so. Nick knew in that moment that he had made the right decision.

His mother would be so proud.

* * *

Isobeille tucked her hand into the crook of Nick's elbow. The strange current flowed through her again, but she was better prepared for it this time. It was a sign, she thought, just like Nick's timely intervention and subsequent return. For whatever reason, it felt right. She was meant to be here, with him.

Mayhap that explained her lack of trepidation. There was a sense of excitement, yes, but no genuine fear. Isobeille decided that any man who had gone to the effort he had to save her from the silver beast deserved a bit of trust. Besides, it wasn't like she had a lot of other options. And he had such kind eyes. The eyes gave the best measure of a man, she thought.

It would behoove her to be on her best behavior, however. To censor her words and curtail her untoward thoughts, lest he decide to abandon her again. Thankfully, he had seen fit to give her another chance. Isobeille did her best to keep her eyes respectfully averted from his, and to do as he commanded without hesitation, for no matter the culture, he was a man, and she, naught but a woman, and a rather helpless one at that.

It *was* difficult, though. So many odd and wondrous things clamored for her attention that she found it nearly impossible to keep her eyes cast downward. Unable to refrain for long, she peeked up a few times, and when Nick showed no sign of displeasure, she gave up entirely. Completely entranced by this new world, she tried to see everything at once.

Wrapped in the fragrant warmth of Nick's sleeved cloak, with the heat of his arm beneath her fingers, she barely noticed the icy nip of the air or the cold stone beneath her feet. They walked along at a fairly brisk pace. Since his legs were so much longer than hers, she was forced to skip to keep up with his strides, at least until he realized what she was doing and slowed down a bit.

She had no idea where they were going, but it mattered not. In her heart of hearts, she knew she was safe with him.

"What do you feel like?" Nick asked. It startled her a bit, caught up as she was in everything else around her. "Burgers? Pizza? Chinese? Sorry, but we're kind of limited to take-out. You're not really dressed for a night on the town."

Isobeille looked down at herself, then at everyone else around them. Granted, she spied no other garments similar to her own, but it was not as if her *legs* were showing (as they were on so many others).

"No shoes," he explained, pointing at her feet after obviously sensing her confusion. "It's against the city health code to go into a restaurant – even a dive – without shoes. It's considered a public health hazard."

She looked doubtfully at one woman whose upper body was wrapped in some kind of fur but was sporting an exceptionally short skirt and walking into what was clearly an eating establishment.

"But baring your arse afore all the world isnae?" she asked before she could stop herself.

Following her eyes, Nick barked out a laugh. "Not if you're wearing shoes."

Chapter 3

They walked the first couple of blocks, but it wasn't easy. In a town where people typically avoided eye contact like the plague, Nick was very aware of the curious looks they were getting (more so Isobeille than him). Those from the men ranged from appreciative to outright creepy; those from the women ranked anywhere from curious to catty.

Isobeille didn't appear to notice any of them. Wide-eyed and curious, her head swiveled as if on a stick. Nick was forced to catch her several times when she stumbled because her eyes were elsewhere, or to hold her back when she attempted to simply walk out into the middle of the street, heedless of the traffic because something else had grabbed her attention.

Eventually he decided it was just too dangerous, and he needed to get her somewhere warm before she got frostbite on those cute little toes.

Nick flagged a cab and guided Isobeille into it. She was hesitant at first. For a few moments it appeared that she would refuse to get in altogether, but Nick managed to coax her in using what his partner had dubbed his "soothing voice", which he used with great success upon frightened, panicked victims. He tried not to think too much about her apparent trust in him, because then he would have to remind himself that she was most likely a few bricks shy of a load to be blindly getting into a car with a stranger in the first place.

"First time in a taxi, I take it?" Nick asked wryly. From the moment the door closed her face had grown increasingly pale and her eyes widened. That, combined with the death grip she had on his arm, gave him his first clue.

"Is that what ye call this beast?" she managed through gritted teeth.

He shook his head, wondering again where in the hell she had come from.

Thankfully, it wasn't a far ride and they arrived at Nick's apartment building without further incident. He paid the driver and pried Isobeille out of the cab. She huddled close to him while he extracted his keys and unlocked the entry door. As she stood on the steps, her skirt held in her hands, he was once again stricken by the sight of her small, delicate feet.

"Why aren't you wearing shoes?" he asked, unable to contain the question any longer.

"A woman cannae wander far without shoes now, can she?" she said with what he could have sworn was a triumphant gleam in her eye, and he couldn't help feeling like he was missing something important.

Shaking his head, he guided her toward the elevator and pushed the up button. After several long moments of waiting, she said, "Not te be ungrateful, but why are we staring at a wall?"

He glanced down, vaguely wondering at how big he felt next to her. "We're not staring at a wall. We're waiting for an elevator. Haven't you ever been in an elevator either?"

Before she could answer, the soft ding announced the arrival of the car. When the doors slid open with a swish, Isobeille jumped back.

"Come on," he coaxed, stepping in and holding the door open with one hand.

"Ye wish me te climb inte a box?" she asked, eyeing the small space with obvious suspicion.

"Fastest way to the seventh floor."

When she remained outside, looking very much like she had when he pushed her into the back of the cab, it finally hit him.

"You're claustrophobic, aren't you?"

She straightened her shoulders and lifted her chin. "I doona ken what that is, but it sounds verra rude."

Nick released the doors and stepped back out into the lobby. "It means you don't like tight, enclosed spaces."

"Aye. I doona."

"Alright, no elevator tonight. We'll take the stairs instead."

The look of relief on her face when the elevator doors closed without them in it almost made the thought of walking seven flights on the heels of a twelve-hour shift worth it. *Almost*.

Nick liked to think he was in fairly decent shape. As a paramedic, being in good physical condition was a definite plus. On any given night he never knew what he was going to have to face. But as they came out on the seventh floor, even he was breathing a little heavily. Isobeille, however, seemed as unaffected as if she had taken the elevator after all. Definitely not as fragile as she looked then, he concluded.

"This is me," he announced when they reached his door. "Come on in." Nick entered first, flicking on the lights as he did so.

Isobeille peeked around the doorframe as if she expected to find another elevator. Even from several feet away her sigh of relief was audible. She stepped over the threshold, her eyes growing wide.

"This is yer home?"

"Yeah. Not much, I know, but it's about all I can afford."

"I think it is wonderful!" she said, turning around full circle.

Nick tossed his keys on the small table by the door. Not for the first time that evening, he questioned the wisdom of bringing a strange woman into his apartment, strange being the operative word. For all of her quirks, however, she seemed harmless enough.

He looked back to where Isobeille remained rooted by the door, her hand poised against the wall.

"It's all right," he said, continuing on further into the apartment. "Come on in and let's - "

Whatever Nick was about to say was cut off as the room fell into sudden and complete darkness. Instinctively, Nick turned and headed back toward where he had last seen her, encountering the solid oak coffee table in the process.

"Damn it! What did you do that for?!?"

Instantly, the entire room was illuminated once again. Nick was several feet in front of her, rubbing his wounded knee. He watched, annoyed, as she hit the switch repeatedly, her eyes looking at each of the lights in turn as they flicked on and off.

"Stop that!" he said, a little too harshly. And it was *not* because she failed to notice that she had caused him injury. He was a better man than that.

"Oh!" she said, looking surprised, as if she had forgotten he was even there. "My apologies! Are ye all right?"

"It's nothing," he said, straightening, his manly pride mollified now that she had recognized his pain. "So what's next? Are you going to tell me you didn't have electricity where you come from either?" he said half-jokingly.

"Nay, we dinnae."

His laughter ceased when he realized she

wasn't kidding. "Hey, what are you, like some kind of Amish or something?" He knew from growing up in central Pennsylvania that there were many pockets of the strict religious community around who shunned anything even remotely technologically advanced, electricity included.

Come to think of it, they didn't dress all that differently either, except he couldn't quite recall such an enticing neckline on any Amish garb he'd ever seen. Maybe she was doing one of the Amish walk-about things, *Rumschpringe* or something like that - where the young ones spent a year exploring the outside world before officially committing to the Amish ways. But they were Pennsylvania Dutch, a.k.a., German, not Celtic, right?

"I amnae *Amish*," she said, though he could tell she didn't really know what that was. "But we dinnae have anything like these magic candles in our village. What was it ye called them? E-lech-trocities?"

Nick blinked, making a conscious effort to close his now-gaping mouth. "Electricity. And if you don't know anything about electricity or cabs or elevators, how did you wind up in the middle of the city?"

She opened her mouth to respond, but he held up his hand. "Wait. Don't tell me just yet. I have a feeling I'm going to need a few drinks first. Let's just get you cleaned up and fed, then we'll hit the heavy stuff, okay?"

She closed her mouth dutifully and nodded.

"Right then. First things first. What are you hungry for? Italian? Chinese? Mexican?"

Isobeille rubbed her arms as she looked around. "Something hot would do quite nicely, thank ye, if 'tis not too much trouble."

"It's all hot," he said, bemused.

Isobeille nibbled that bottom lip again. She probably didn't even realize she was doing it, but that tiny gesture had a far more significant impact than it should have on him, playing havoc with some of his baser male instincts.

"What would ye choose?"

"I'm partial to pizza myself."

"Then I, too, would like *peetzuhm*. If ye tell me how te make it, I will be most happy te prepare it for ye."

Nick blinked. "I don't want you to make it," he clarified, grabbing the phone and tapping in the number from memory. "I'm going to have it delivered."

He spoke briefly into the phone, watching as she reached out and tentatively stroked the top of his leather recliner with her finger, then her whole hand. Like the lip-chewing thing, it shouldn't have affected him, but it did. As he slipped his phone back into his pocket, he shifted discreetly and told himself to get a grip.

"Food should be here in about forty-five minutes. That'll give you plenty of time to freshen up, then I'll take a better look at that hand."

"'Tis fine," she said quickly, pushing her arm behind her.

"I'll be the judge of that. It is kind of what I do." He paused, hands on hips, not quite believing what he was going to ask her next. But then again, if she didn't know about cabs or pizza or electricity, maybe it wasn't so unreasonable.

"Uh, not to sound insulting or anything, but do you know how to use the bathroom?"

Another blank look. "Ye have a separate room for a bath?"

Yep. Not unreasonable at all. "Right. Come on, then. I'm going to give you a crash course in modern bathroom facilities."

Sufficiently satisfied that she had the gist of the workings of indoor plumbing (and after discreetly removing all sharp or harmful objects from the immediate vicinity) he left her in the bathroom with some spare clothes Gloria kept at his place. Shaking his head and grinning at her occasional squeals of delight – apparently she had figured out the pulsing massage setting on the shower head by the sounds of it - he cracked open a cold beer and tried to figure out just what the hell had happened to him in the last hour.

Chapter 4

Isobeille squealed when she turned the smooth silver handle, effectively dousing herself in the process. She looked up into the circular device above her head with awe. How could such a relatively small thing hold so much rain?

And to draw forth heated water *instantly*? 'Twas far better than collecting from the cistern, bucket by bucket, and heating it over the hearth. One could bathe *standing up*, and did not even need to dispose of the dirty water afterward, she mused, watching it as it drained away between her feet. Where exactly did it go?

No less impressive was the gleaming white, oddly-shaped chamber pot bolted to the floor. She had been just about to ask Nick how one emptied such a thing earlier, but then he had pushed down upon a lever and *whoosh*! With barely concealed joy, Isobeille *flushed* it again several times, grinning in delight as she watched the water swirl downward and the bowl magically fill up again.

And the light *switches*, as he had called them. How clever was that? Located in each separate chamber, she was fascinated by them. Isobeille reached out and touched it with her finger, just as she had seen him do. Immediately, the small garderobe was plunged into darkness. With one more flick, she was once again bathed in light.

It was all so amazing! Not just the hot water and instant light, but everything she had encountered thus far. When Nick had first ushered her inside his home, she had not known what to expect, but it was nothing short of miraculous. She had seen the tall structures from the outside, of course, but never in a hundred years could she have imagined this. Each large box was divided up into many smaller boxes - homes stacked on top of and next to each other. How very clever!

She looked up warily, a brief flash of panic at the realization that there were more such places on top of her even now, but then forced that thought aside. Obviously it was safe enough if the city was filled with such dwellings.

She had so much to learn about this new world! Her fingers were itching to touch and explore all of the amazing colors and textures around her, but she was averse to keeping her host waiting too long. If she could manage not to anger him, perhaps she would have ample opportunity to further explore and discover more later.

With that in mind, Isobeille lifted one of the garments he had requested she wear. Holding it in front of her, she twisted it this way and that, wrinkling her nose. Trews? Apparently, it was customary for women to dress in such a way in this strange and wondrous realm - she had seen as much out in the street – but she herself had never done so.

She shrugged and began to remove her shabby gown. Changing into more acceptable clothing seemed a small enough concession for Nick's kindness. If this is what he wished, she would at least make an effort to please him.

* * *

Nick was halfway through his second beer when the delivery guy appeared. In a classic case of poor timing, Isobeille chose that moment to emerge from the bathroom. Without turning around, Nick knew that it could not be good. The open-mouthed gawk of the nineteen-year-old in his doorway told him as much.

Steeling himself, Nick turned and swallowed hard at the sight before him. There was Isobeille, in vivid glory. Her towel-damp, glorious curls cascaded down to her hips, a shade of dark red that glistened like a shiny candy apple under the lights. The jeans he had provided were several inches too long at the bottom and too narrow at the waist, requiring that the zipper be left hanging open. If that wasn't bad enough, the designer T was at least two sizes too small, accentuating substantial breasts and revealing a fair part of her midsection.

He swallowed hard. Forget the St. Paulie girl. She looked like the quintessential poster ad for Hooters.

"Nick, I doona think I did this right," she said simply.

"Fuck me," the delivery boy murmured, and Nick was forced to agree with his assessment. In her costume dress, she had been sexy. In tight jeans and T-shirt, she was nothing short of drool-worthy.

Shaking himself free of the erotic images now dancing in his head, he hastily paid the kid and pushed him out the door. Tossing the pizza to the side, Nick then proceeded to take Isobeille by the arm and lead her back toward his bedroom. He would never manage to get anything past the constriction in his throat if he didn't do *something*.

He rummaged in his drawer for a minute, trying desperately to ignore the way Isobeille was feeling up the down comforter and the fluffy pillows on his bed, mumbling to himself until he extracted a pair of gray sweats and an old football practice jersey. He placed both in her hands.

"Try these instead," he said, wishing his voice didn't sound like he'd just swallowed a cup of ground glass. Then he left, closing the door firmly behind him.

He would *not* think of how much bigger her breasts were than Gloria's, nor the contours of her perfect heart-shaped ass. He would *not* think of how good she smelled, or how soft and utterly lickable her creamy skin looked. And he would *not*, under any circumstances, consider the kinds of sounds she might make as he buried himself repeatedly in her lush little body or screamed out his name in that thick brogue of hers.

He had a girlfriend, goddammit. A girlfriend who he would be with *right now* had he not been running late. If he had picked Gloria up on time, she never would have been in her little cubicle when the editor came by with an extra assignment, and he wouldn't be pacing back and forth in his tiny living room sporting the hard-on from hell.

Was it unusually hot in the apartment? It sure felt hot. Nick exhaled heavily and checked the thermostat, which displayed a completely illogical seventy-one degrees. That was obviously not right. Nick made a mental note to call the building super first thing in the morning and get it checked out.

In the meantime, he pulled his thermal over his head, leaving him in his plain white, short-sleeved cotton T and went back to the problem at hand.

What was he thinking about again? Oh, right. *Gloria.*

At least she hadn't sounded too pissed that he'd blown their date. Nick wasn't quite sure what that meant, exactly. Maybe Gloria was glad for the opportunity to get a little extra credit. Her job and her career were very important to her; she was always trying to suck up (though she preferred to call it 'capitalizing on an opportunity to advance her career').

Or maybe Gloria was glad for the chance to put things off between them for a little while longer. Hadn't she told him that she wanted to keep things from getting too complicated too quickly? That she needed 'space' and 'time' to 'discover who she was' before she could even think about committing to something more than the occasional, albeit exclusive, hook-up?

He would have to wait and see; the answers weren't going to magically come to him tonight, and he had other, more pressing issues to deal with at that moment. In any event, Nick had managed to wrestle his hormones back under some semblance of control by the time Isobeille emerged from his bedroom.

"Does this please ye better?" she asked doubtfully.

He brought his hand up to his mouth to try to hide the smile he could not completely contain. Tiny feet peeked out from beneath his baggy sweats, rolled up several times at the ankle. His old jersey hung to her knees, but sufficiently covered all of those tempting curves from view.

Thank God.

"Infinitely," he said, breathing a sigh of relief. "Now let's take a look at that hand, then we can eat."

Nick was acutely aware of Isobeille's gaze as

he examined her hand. As a paramedic, he was used to all sorts of reactions from the patients he treated. Some were grateful, some were scared, some were just plain nasty. Occasionally he would feel the heat of a woman's stare (or less commonly, a man's) as he tended to their injuries. But none of them seemed to affect him quite as strongly as Isobeille's. It felt warm, like the sun on his skin, and sank down deep into his bones (and various other body parts).

Outwardly, he remained coolly professional. But inside his chest, his heart pounded out a thunderous tattoo. A viscous warmth spread from where he held her hand in his, travelled up his arm and into his chest, settling somewhere around his midsection. This time, he didn't bother checking the thermostat.

And it wasn't just her tangible gaze or the blossoming warmth from holding her hand that was messing with his senses – it was her scent, too. With each breath he took, he drew in the scent of fresh snow and wildflowers. He had to wonder where the hell that came from, because he couldn't think of a single product in his bathroom that smelled like that. Maybe Gloria had left something.

Then again, Gloria never smelled like *this*. Like nature at its finest.

"Ye have a gentle touch for such a strong mon," she said softly, bringing his ears into the sensory party. The only thing left was taste, and he was so not going there. "Are ye a healer?"

A healer? "Sort of, I guess. I'm a paramedic." When she didn't seem to know what that was (and why was he not surprised?) he explained simply, "When there's an accident or someone is hurt, my job is to assess their injuries and treat them until we can get them to a hospital."

She smiled at him as if he had just told her he'd hung the stars in the sky. "Ye help people."

Nick felt his cheeks burning. Jesus, was he blushing? "It's no big deal."

"Aye, 'tis," she insisted, her smile growing wider.

He decided to drop it, focusing on coating a few of the deeper scratches with some antibiotic cream and applying some band-aids. She seemed legitimately impressed with him, yes, and that made him feel pretty good, at least until he remembered that she'd been pretty damn impressed with a light switch and a flushing toilet, too.

* * *

Isobeille studied him closely as he took a slice of pizza and bit into it, intending to mimic his actions. She had done the same with the bottle of beer he had given her, lifting it to her lips and tilting her head backward (she likened it to a weak but pleasant ale). For some reason, he seemed to find it amusing. His kind brown eyes held flecks of gold that sparkled when he laughed; it required deliberate effort on her part not to lose herself in them entirely.

Forcing her eyes away, she focused on the triangular-shaped food in front of her instead. Carefully lifting it to her mouth, Isobeille took the first bite. Her eyes widened as the combination of spicy, cheesy flavors exploded against her taste buds. She savored it, then swallowed and eagerly took another bite.

"Good?" he asked as she polished off her piece and tried to discreetly lick her fingers.

"'Tis the most delicious fare I have ever tasted!" she proclaimed. "May I have more?"

"Absolutely," he grinned back, nudging the box closer to her. "So. How about telling me who you are and why you're in New York?"

Isobeille extracted a slice and set it upon the thin, lightweight trencher he had provided. Her voracious appetite faded somewhat when she realized the time had come to give him the answers he wanted. Mayhap it was just as well; she had a few questions of her own.

"Is that what ye call this place? New Yorick?"

"New *York*. And you're obviously not from around here."

"Nay, I amnae." She paused, taking the time to carefully chew and swallow as she considered her next words. "I doona wish te lie te ye, Nick, as ye have been verra kind, but I doona ken if the truth is what ye really want te hear."

"What makes you think I wouldn't want to hear the truth?"

She gave him a nervous smile. "I fear ye will think me a wee bit daft."

"Sweetheart, I already think you're a little daft. The first time I saw you, you were smack-dab in the middle of the street about to do the horizontal tango with a ten-ton bus, barefoot and dressed like a Braveheart extra. And nothing I've seen since then has done anything to tip the scales into the rational zone."

"Ye do make a fine point," she agreed, even though she hadn't understood half of what he said. "All right then, I will tell ye my tale, and hope that ye doona see fit te stone me."

Nick nodded encouragingly, holding up both hands. "Go on. No stones, I promise."

"A few sennights past, I accompanied my father to the Michaelmas celebration in the nearest village to our home, Gwynnevael."

"Michaelmas?" Nick interrupted. "Is that like Christmas?"

"Michaelmas is a feast in celebratory remembrance of the Archangels. 'Tis named for Michael especially, ye ken, because he is the greatest of the Archangels for defeating Lucifer and all."

"Got it," he nodded. "Go on."

"Weel, 'tis a verra important time, marking the

end of the harvest and the beginning of the year's accounts. All debts have te be settled by the end of the celebration, ye ken, and my Da couldnae make the reckoning."

"Sir Galen was at the festival as weel, and saw the bind that my Da had gotten himself inte. He offered te settle my father's debts in return for my hand."

Nick shifted on the sofa. "Wait – are you telling me that your father sold you to dig himself out of a financial hole?"

Isobeille winced. "'Tis not quite that simple, but aye, that is the gist of it." She took a drink from the bottle before continuing.

"Sir Galen is a fine and decent mon te be sure, a celebrated knight with many commendations for courage and bravery."

"That doesn't sound so bad," Nick said.

"Nay, it doesnae," she agreed. "A woman could do far worse than Sir Galen, even though he is closer te my father's age than my own. 'Tis not unusual for an older man te desire a younger bride, and Sir Galen made no secret of the fact that he wanted a hale young wife te breed his heirs."

"I can see where you might have a problem with that. I guess saying no wasn't an option?"

Isobeille shook her head and chanced a look at Nick, expecting to see censure or at least disapproval on his face, but found none. Was it possible that he might be able to empathize with her desire not to marry the knight?

"I went te Sir Galen when my Da was deep in his cups and begged him te take me inte indentured service instead te pay off my father's debt, but he wouldnae hear of it." She dropped her gaze in embarrassment. "He said he wanted te give me something better than a life of servitude. He dinnae ken that for me, 'twas not all that different."

"What about your father? Did you try talking to him?"

"Aye," she nodded, "till I was blue about the lips, but all that got me was the back of his hand and a week's worth of bruises."

"Your father hit you?" Nick stiffened beside her; his voice had gone deep and quiet.

"'Twas not unusual," she said matter-of-factly. "He is fond of the drink, ye ken. I am told he was a great mon once, respected among his people."

"What changed?"

"My mother died upon the childbed. I doona think he has ever quite forgiven me for that. He loved her verra much."

Nick gaped at her. "How could he possibly hold you accountable for that? It wasn't your fault, Isobeille. Sometimes bad stuff just happens."

"Mayhap, but I dinnae help matters. I tried te be a dutiful daughter, but dinnae always do as I should, and men doona want a disobedient woman. Unmarried at four and twenty like an old maid! I am naught but an embarrassment te him, and I think he was glad te finally find a mon willing te have me. Te gain some coin was a fine bonus as weel."

When Nick said nothing more, Isobeille sighed, interpreting his silence for agreement. "I dinnae want te wed Sir Galen, nor did I wish te remain under my father's hand. I ken 'tis wrong of me te wish for such things, but upon return te the village from the great feast 'tis exactly what I did. Each night, as I awaited Sir Galen te return for me, I sat beneath the stars and prayed for deliverance. 'Twas on my last night when I suddenly felt verra drowsy. I must have fallen asleep, and when I awoke, ye were saving me from the great silver beast."

Chapter 5

It took a moment for Nick to realize she was talking about the bus, and with that realization came a flood of impossibilities, hitting him fast and hard.

"Isobeille," Nick said slowly, keeping his voice calm and level, "what year was it when you fell asleep?"

"'Twas the year of our Lord, 1414."

Nick blinked. He took a breath, letting that sink in. It wasn't really as much of a shock as it should have been. Maybe he'd already been thinking somewhere along those lines way back in the far recesses of his mind, where things like time travel and great silvery dragons were still remote possibilities.

A long silence stretched between them, with only the muted sounds of the busy street far below to fill in the space.

"I have already figured out that I am no longer in that time," she finally said quietly. "May I inquire as te what year it is here?"

Nick's brown eyes met hers. "2014."

Isobeille inhaled sharply, no doubt doing the calculations in her head. "I have travelled six hundred years through time?" she asked, her voice a bit weak and shaky.

"It would appear so." Nick tilted the bottle and drained the last of his beer, infinitely glad he'd had the foresight to postpone this little chat until after his stomach was full and he'd kicked back a few. He felt surprisingly calm, considering.

"Ye are taking this verra well," Isobeille said carefully, mirroring his thoughts. "Do ye think I am daft?"

"Honestly? I'm not sure what to believe. It all seems pretty... incredible." *Understatement of the year, that*, sniped a slightly dazed (and perhaps buzzed) part of his brain.

"Aye, that it does," she agreed. "But do ye no' believe that sometimes prayers are answered?"

Did he? It was a legitimate question. He'd grown up going to church every Sunday, doing the Sunday school thing, learned all about faith and prayers and mysterious ways. It was his job, though – the shit he saw every day - that really put his faith to the test.

After a couple of years of arriving at nearly every kind of horrific scene imaginable, he felt pretty secure in the knowledge that there was a higher power at work, though he was a little fuzzy on the level of involvement, especially when it came to things like personalized prayers. Some people, it seemed, had guardian angels looking out for them. Others, not so much. And then there was the whole "be careful what you wish for" scenario, which seemed to describe Isobeille's situation perfectly.

"Sure," he answered finally, "but I'm not sure I'd consider being picked up out of my own time and dropped in front of a cross-town bus a *good* thing."

To his surprise, Isobeille laughed, lifting some of the heaviness that seemed to have settled over them.

"The Lord works in mysterious ways. Mayhap I was put there for a purpose."

"What possible purpose could God have for placing you in the path of almost certain death?" Nick honestly wasn't trying to be a smart-ass. It was a valid question.

Isobeille considered that for a moment. "Weel, had I not been placed there at that verra moment, ye wouldnae have saved me."

Her words rang like the finest crystal throughout his head. "Are you suggesting –"

"I amnae suggesting anything," she said, laying her hand upon his arm, sending ripples of warmth into him before she realized what she was doing and pulled her hand away. He had the sudden urge to take her hand and put it right back where it was.

"Nor would I presume te think I ken what the Lord intended. I am only telling ye the truth as ye asked and as I said I would."

She was so different from anyone he had ever met. So... *unjaded.* Yet if everything she told him was true, she had every right to be copping a major attitude. Beaten by her father? Sold into marriage? Dropped barefoot and vulnerable into one of the toughest cities in the world six hundred years in the future? He'd be pissed off as hell.

But Isobeille didn't seem angry at all. If anything she was handling this all remarkably well, with grace and gratitude.

"Fair enough. Hey, for what it's worth, I don't think it's wrong of you to want more."

She smiled serenely. "Thank ye, Nick. Ye are a verra good mon te be doing all this for a woman ye dinnae ken."

He wasn't sure how to respond to that, so he settled for giving her hand a little squeeze. It was weird, but helping Isobeille really didn't feel like it was all that much of a hardship. Isobeille was sweet, intelligent, naïve, gentle. The word "docile" came to mind instantly, and it fit surprisingly well. Nick ignored the stirrings within, certain that they were only a natural reaction to all the things she had told him.

Those unfamiliar feelings didn't mean anything. Especially when Nick had always been attracted to strong, independent women as a general rule. But inside, he was still a man. And surely any man would feel that tug of want to protect her, keep her safe, show her that there were some decent people still left in the world.

Right?

They cleaned up together, avoiding any more

talk of Isobeille's past by mutual, silent agreement. Isobeille insisted on doing the dishes since Nick provided dinner. He tried to explain that ordering pizza really wasn't a big deal, but she was having none of it. She was so thrilled with the sink and the concept of running water – not to mention the dish soap and the bubbles it made – that he didn't have the heart to refuse. Instead he just grabbed a towel and helped. It was kind of nice, he thought, doing something incredibly normal in the midst of so much weirdness.

"So I have been yammering all night," she said, blowing another blast of bubbles into the air and grinning as she watched them drift slowly back down to the counter. "Tell me of yer beloved."

"Gloria?" Funny, he really hadn't thought much about her all night.

"Aye. She is verra lucky te gain the attention of such a mon as yerself. I would wager she is bonnie, isnae she?"

"She is beautiful," he agreed. "And smart. She's apprenticing for a major newspaper while working on her Master's."

"She has a master?" Isobeille asked. "Is she indentured, then?"

Isobeille was so easy to be around that he was finding it hard to remember that she was from an entirely different world (at least theoretically). He patiently explained that a Master's degree was a form of higher education. She was greatly impressed.

"Ah, what a wonderful age," she sighed wistfully. "That women can earn a wage and be schooled. Can they own land, then, too?"

He laughed, though inside he was still feeling a little shaken. "Yes. Women can do anything men do. If someone tells a woman she can't do something simply because of her gender, it's called discrimination, and it's against the law."

"Verily?" She asked, incredulous. It seemed a small thing to believe, especially to a woman who expected him to accept that she had time-travelled from medieval Scotland, but what did he know?

All too soon the dishes were done and Nick couldn't think of a good enough reason to keep her awake any longer, especially when she looked like she was about to fall over from sheer exhaustion. After retrieving pillows and blankets and making up the sofa for her (she threatened to leave if Nick insisted upon her having his bed even once more), he reluctantly bid her a good night and headed into his bedroom.

Well, that explained why she wasn't wearing shoes, he thought later as he lay in his bed staring up at the ceiling. Her father must have sensed how unhappy Isobeille was; the man required her to give them to him whenever he went anywhere, reasoning that without shoes she would be less likely to run off. Strange how it was that thought that struck him out of everything else he had heard. His head was still spinning.

Nick set his mind on a mental replay, reviewing what had to be the most bizarre evening in his entire life. Despite the fact that he had been an active participant, it was still difficult to wrap his mind around it. It read like the rejected outline of a *Back To The Future* script, or maybe a *Dr. Who* episode:

1. Save hot Scottish chick from certain death. *Check.*
2. Bring said Scottish chick home. *Check.*
3. Share pizza and beer with Scottish chick. *Check.*
4. Discuss time travel and her life in 15th century Scotland. *Check.*

The scariest part of all? He believed her.

There wasn't any one thing that made him decide that Isobeille was not completely batshit insane as he had originally feared. It was the whole package, really. Her manner of dressing. Her speech. Her total cluelessness about the world around her. The look that she had given him after that first bite of pizza – the one that made him feel like he'd just given her a box of diamonds instead of a Mario's Pepperoni and Extra Cheese.

Nobody was that good of an actress, especially since he could actually feel her emotions as she spun her story. And what a story!

What was perhaps even harder to stomach than

the whole travelling through time thing was the thought that anyone could treat Isobeille that way. Sure, he'd only known her for a few hours, but it had been enough for him to know that she was quite possibly the sweetest, most compliant woman he'd ever met. That might also go a long way in explaining why he felt so protective of her all of a sudden, or the irrational anger he'd tried so hard to hide as she told her tale.

Especially when she brought up the stoning thing at the very beginning. He had been only marginally sure that she was joking about that, but now he wasn't so sure at all. *Jesus*. Did they really do that kind of thing? Then again, if he remembered his history correctly, up until a couple hundred years ago, most cultures had some pretty brutal ways of dealing with anything out of the ordinary.

There was absolutely nothing ordinary about Isobeille or the things she had told him.

Like when she'd been talking about her life, and why she hadn't fit in. Nick had been so flabbergasted by her words that he couldn't respond. Old maid? Unwanted? Disobedient? What kind of people could ever view her like that, freaking idiots?

And what was the deal with her old man? It was hard to get past the fact that a father would try to sell his daughter, especially one as seemingly sweet and gentle as Isobeille. At the same time he had to wonder what kind of man would "buy" a girl like Isobeille. He absently totaled the cash in his wallet and the little bit he had in the bank, wondering if it would have been enough...

Maybe the knight really wasn't such a bad guy; maybe he, like Nick, had seen his protective instincts rise to the surface and thought he could offer her something better. It still didn't excuse the whole ownership thing or the breeding of heirs, however. Obviously, based on the little he knew about Isobeille so far, wherever she was from was pretty old-school in terms of technological advances. And clothing. But backwards village or not, that shit just wasn't right.

Nick exhaled heavily. Why the hell did he even care so much?

Maybe it was the approaching holiday that was making him so sentimental. Or maybe it was the fact that he was feeling a little lost himself these days. Whatever the reason, he definitely felt a strange connection to this peculiar woman, and it wasn't unpleasant.

The irresistible urge to see her again gripped him, though he had only left her barely an hour ago. Maybe he just needed to ensure that she really did exist, that he hadn't made the whole thing up in his own mind.

Exiting his bedroom quietly so as not to wake her, he looked to the couch. His heart dropped when he saw the pillows and blanket scrunched up in the corner, the irrational thought that maybe he should have thought to have taken her shoes, too, popping into his mind before remembering she didn't have any to begin with. Then his gaze was drawn to the window, where Isobeille sat in the deep sill, her knees drawn up close to her chest, staring out into the night. With her hair loose and sleep-tussled and wearing his oversized college football practice jersey, she was quite possibly the most adorable looking creature he'd ever seen. Would have been, if he hadn't seen the incredibly lost expression reflected back at him in the glass.

"Can't sleep?" he asked finally, because it was impossible to remain on the far side of the room any longer. She was like a powerful magnet, drawing him closer.

She shook her head. "My apologies. I dinnae mean te wake ye."

"You didn't. I'm having a little trouble nodding off myself."

He moved slowly toward the window, wanting to be close but not to crowd her. They remained in companionable silence for a little while. Lying in bed, Nick had thought of a hundred different things to ask her, but he suddenly found himself at a loss, unable to think of a single one. Instead, he contented himself with simply keeping her company.

It was no hardship. The moonlight cast a silvery glow over her dark red locks, making them look as if they were covered in fairy dust (or what he imagined fairy dust would look like based on years of Disney animation).

"It must be hard for you," he said finally. "To process all this, I mean." To be in one world – the only one you had ever known – one minute, in a completely different world the next – it was beyond his immediate comprehension. While lying in bed and thinking upon all that she had told him, he came to the conclusion that he would not have handled the situation nearly as well. Hell, he probably would have jumped through that window by now, instead of just staring out through it.

She didn't answer right away; he thought maybe she wouldn't. He was about to go back to his room and leave her to her thoughts when she said, "Nay so much as ye might imagine. Truth be told, I dinnae really feel much a part of my old world, either. I amnae verra good at doing what I am told and have an unnatural curiosity about things, ye ken. Both are poor qualities for a woman te have."

She turned briefly, offering him a slight, sad smile. "I even managed te rile ye a few times, and ye are mayhap the kindest mon I have ever met. I but wonder if there is anywhere I do belong."

When had she riled him? He frowned, thinking over the events of the evening. His first words to her had been yelled into her face. Granted, he hadn't known then what he knew now (or thought he knew), but that just made the fact that she'd trusted him so completely that much more incredible. She must have been scared witless as it was, but then to find herself tackled by some guy and yelled at and dragged through a world that had to have been nothing less than terrifying to her? It boggled the mind.

In his defense, though, it *was* better than getting flattened by a bus.

"Come here," he said, coaxing her onto the sofa with him. After a moment's hesitation, she left her perch and slid down beside him. His arm went around her shoulders and she leaned tentatively against him. He ignored the sense of rightness that flooded through him, noting that it was just a natural reaction to doing something good for someone in trouble. Those kinds of feel-good vibes are what prompted him to become a paramedic in the first place, or so he told himself.

"I've been thinking about what you said," he said quietly. "About Fate or God or whatever put you here, in this place, in this time, for a very specific reason. And I think you were right. You belong here, Isobeille."

He didn't say so, but he was thinking about himself, too. If he hadn't felt the overwhelming need to help out at that accident at the end of the day, he wouldn't have been running late, he wouldn't have missed his date with Gloria, and he wouldn't have been in the right place and time to keep Isobeille from being hit by the bus.

And she wouldn't be next to him right now.

Her response was a soft sigh. Nick continued to hold her, trying not to think about just how perfectly she fit against him, or how right she felt beneath his arm. It was only a byproduct of circumstance, nothing more.

"But what will I do?" she asked. "It appears that I had not given much thought te what might happen if my prayers were indeed answered. I suppose that shows a great lack of faith on my part."

"We'll figure something out," he said, stroking her hair as if it was the most natural thing in the world to do. Before long, her breathing became deep and rhythmic, and he knew she had finally fallen asleep.

Grabbing a throw, he covered them both and leaned back, easing her with him gently so he would not wake her. He yawned, feeling warm and strangely content. As his eyes began to close of their own accord, he promised himself he'd go back to his own room in a few minutes…

Chapter 6

Nick was reminded of his youth as he rose slowly from the depths of perfect slumber. Feeling incredibly warm and comfortable, with none of the usual aches and pains, he felt almost weightless. For those few moments, it was as if all was right with his world. There was no grogginess, no dread in facing his day, no stress over yet another poor night's sleep or worry over his job or Gloria or anything else for that matter. It was as if it had all been sucked away, leaving him pleasantly content and almost … happy.

What the hell?

A soft female sigh and the sensation of slight movement along the length of his body immediately launched him from his exquisite lassitude into hyper awareness.

His hand ventured forth in stealthy exploration, mapping out soft, full curves. Not Gloria, his brain instantly announced. His cock stood straight up and bobbed beneath his loose pajama bottoms, and in his mind Nick heard the very clear message from his groin: *I could have told you that.*

He was hard. No, that wasn't quite accurate.

He was industrial-grade, *granite* hard. With his other hand – the one currently not overflowing with lush ripe female flesh – he touched himself lightly. Even that slight contact nearly had him howling with desperate, visceral need.

Moist breath blew across his chest, along with another shift that had his balls getting in on the act, too. He couldn't remember waking up this jacked-up, all hot need and aching lust. Who the hell -

Isobeille.

Nick extracted himself as quickly and quietly as possible, his body protesting all the way. As he tucked the blanket around her, she turned, reaching for him.

"Nick," she murmured in her sleep, her voice husky and sounding *almost* as needy as he felt.

"Sssshhh," he said in a hushed (and slightly panicked) whisper. "I'm here. Go back to sleep."

She sighed and snuggled into the couch, gripping the small throw pillow like a lifeline. Nick watched, afraid to breathe, until her features relaxed and she fell back into slumber. Then he made a beeline for his bathroom.

Feeling like an adolescent, he snapped the lock on the door into place even as he dropped his PJ's. Throwing his head back, he bit his bottom lip and gave one, two, three hard pulls before he exploded.

It should have helped. It didn't. Only after another round and a really, really cold shower did he successfully manage to get himself to the point where he could safely zip up his jeans. As he leaned his head against the door and summoned the courage to emerge and face his guest, there were only three words capable of accurately describing his frame of mind: *What. The. Fuck.*

* * *

Isobeille awoke in a nest of comfort: soft, cushiony pillows beside and below her, thick fluffy material all around her. It was nothing like her thin straw mattress and coarse animal hair blanket back home.

Nor did she awaken cold and stiff as she normally did. She was cocooned in warmth, and even when she cast off the coverings, the chill blast she had expected did not come. As her feet hit the floor, her toes curled into plush fibers, not the hard dirt and stone to which she was accustomed.

"Good morning." The warm male voice curled around her. Even slightly rough as it was, it was infinitely smoother than her father's whiskey-ravaged tones. Deep and resonant, it instantly soothed her, made her feel safe and protected.

Nick.

"A good morn te ye, as weel," she replied as she stretched.

"Sleep well?"

"Aye, verra. I cannae remember when I have slept quite so weel and deep."

For the first time in a long time, she had not spent the night hovering on the edge of slumber, awaiting even the slightest indication that her father was returning drunk and of a mind to remind her of what her very existence had cost him. Nor had there been any of the nightmares that normally plagued her when her body became so exhausted she had no other choice but to give in to the pull of sleep.

Isobeille padded into the kitchen area and eased up onto one of the two stools set against the small breakfast counter. Nick wore the same kind of pants she'd seen him in the night before, but these were slightly more faded and clung to his form a bit more than the others, offering her a fine view of his muscular thighs and well-sculpted behind. Only when the sudden and unexpected heat began blooming in her core did she realize she been ogling him and forced her eyes elsewhere.

Unfortunately, perusing the rest of him did nothing to assuage her attraction. His feet were bare, and the heavy flannel shirt he wore only accentuated his broad back and shoulders. Dark hair, damp from his shower, curled slightly at the ends, drew her attention to the dark shadow along his jawline. He was, quite simply, the handsomest man she had ever seen.

She added that to the list of characteristics she had assigned him in her mind, having already come to the conclusion that he was the nicest, the kindest, and the most generous. She would do best to guard her heart, she realized, for it was already trying to slip away.

"Well, travelling six hundred years through time will do that to you," he said, turning to smile at her over his shoulder.

Whether it was the words he spoke or the smile he gave her, Isobeille felt her heart squeeze with hope. Squashing down her personal feelings toward her bonnie rescuer, she concentrated on his latest words instead.

"Ye believe me?" Isobeille had been afraid that after some rest and a chance to think upon her tale, he might just decide she was thoroughly daft after all.

"Aye. I mean, yes," he grinned. "Are you hungry?"

Delicious aromas filled the air around her; not all were from the meal he was preparing. "I shouldnae be after making such a right pig of myself yestereve, but aye."

"Good, because I made way more than I can eat myself. Do you want some coffee?"

"Aye." She had no idea what coffee was, but if Nick thought she should have some, she would trust his judgment. He moved around the kitchen comfortably, pouring a dark liquid into a cup and placing it before her.

"Why are you looking at me like that?" he asked.

Isobeille realized she had been staring and turned her attention to the small, ceramic mug before her.

"I have never known a mon te do for himself when there is a woman te do for him." She sipped the coffee and scrunched up her nose at the bitter taste.

"Things are different in my world." He added generous amounts of cream and sugar to her coffee, then pointed to it. "Try it now."

She lifted the cup and took another sip. This time she smiled. "Aye, they are at that."

* * *

Nick wasn't sure if he should be insulted by her generalized comments about men and their self-reliance issues or not. Then he took one look at her guileless face and determined that Isobeille probably didn't even know how to be insulting.

And thank God she'd moved away from the window. When she'd stretched like that and the sun had shone through his worn jersey, revealing the outline of all those curves that had been pressed against him last night... well, for a few minutes there, he thought he was going to have to excuse himself. He was definitely going to find her something heavier for her to wear tonight if he was to have any hope of retaining his sanity.

Which was something they needed to discuss.

Over plates of pancakes, maple syrup, and bacon, Nick broached the subject. "I've been giving it a lot of thought, and I think you should stay here. At least until we come up with a better plan." He sipped his coffee, closely watching her reaction.

If his gaze hadn't been so fixed on her, he might have missed the brief but brilliant flash of hope in her eyes before she managed to mask it. It bothered him a little that she felt the need to do so, but given all that she had revealed the night before, he couldn't really blame her, either.

Isobeille set her fork down gently and dabbed at her lips with the napkin. Medieval she might be, but her table manners were impeccable.

"Ye are verra kind, Nick, but ye have done so much already."

He hadn't been kidding when he said he'd been giving the matter a lot of thought. That had been practically *all* he'd been able to think about since his early morning rise-and-jack routine. Something about this woman was messing with all of his circuits, but it was his common sense and his libido that seemed most affected at present.

He had debated both sides as he showered, dressed, and watched her sleep before deciding to make breakfast. The practical, realistic side of him noted that he had done his good deed, and had satisfied his sense of common decency and his innate human compassion. He should be taking the next logical step, which would be to get her out of his place and somewhere where she could move on (with help, of course).

The impractical and illogical side of him crossed its arms and pouted at that idea. It didn't want Isobeille to go. Despite the near-certain trouble it would bring him, he liked having her around. Of course, these selfish thoughts were wrapped up and neatly hidden beneath various layers of rationalizations for why it really was in her best interest to stay here with him.

"It's not like you have a lot of options, Isobeille. I mean, where else would you go?"

The effect was instantaneous. Isobeille stiffened and sat up a little straighter, followed by the now-familiar defiant tilt to her chin, the one she effected every time he said something that ruffled her feathers. He was no psychologist, but he could guess that it probably had something to do with the fact that her whole life had been a series of limited options.

"I could go te one of those shelters ye told me aboot."

Nick was shaking his head before she even finished getting the words out. Sweet, innocent Isobeille in a place like that, with drug addicts and indigents and prostitutes? Not happening, not if he had anything to say about it.

And he had plenty to say.

"I've been thinking about that, too. I don't think that's a good idea. They'll ask you all kinds of questions, and if you tell them what you told me, they'll put you in a psych ward somewhere. No, you're better off here with me till we can figure something out."

"Psych ward?"

"Crazy house. Looney bin. Insane asylum. Just because I believe you doesn't mean anyone else will."

She paled visibly. Nick didn't like scaring her, but she had to understand what she would face if she decided to strike out on her own. "At the very least, they'll assume you're some kind of illegal alien and have you deported."

"Deported?"

"Shipped out of the country. Besides, you have no identification, no money, no - "

"I have money," she interrupted.

"What?"

"Money. I assume ye mean coin? Aye, I have some." She disappeared into the back, returning with her dress. Reaching into a hidden inner pocket, she first extracted the two twenties he'd handed her the night before, then a small pouch. She tipped the small goatskin bag over the table, sending several gleaming, roughly circular items clattering onto the surface.

Nick looked down at the slightly-irregular objects. He picked up one with a silvery-gray color;

it felt surprisingly heavy in his hand. One side held the engraved profile of a king holding a scepter; the other, a long cross with some writing and symbols he didn't recognize.

* * *

"My dowry," Isobeille said, embarrassed by the small amount, knowing it was not enough to tempt any but the poorest of men. "I took te hiding it so my father wouldnae squander it on drinking and whoring."

An unreadable expression crossed his face. Isobeille did not know if it was due to her raw words or the realization that he held ancient currency in his hand. Mayhap it was a bit of both.

"As cool as this is, it's not going to buy you much as is. I bet a museum would probably pay good money to get their hands on these – Christ, they're in mint condition – but you can't just walk in there with a bag of them. They'd want to know where you'd gotten them, and you can't exactly tell them, can you?"

Isobeille's last hope drained away as the truth of his words sank in. He was right, of course, but it seemed terribly cruel to come this far, to be so close to realizing her dream of having the freedom to make her own choices, only to discover that she was really not very close at all.

In a way, she was even farther away than she

had been in Gwynnevael. She knew not enough of the customs of this complicated society to do anything on her own. Without Nick's aid, she was all but helpless.

"Are you in such a hurry to leave, Isobeille?" Nick asked quietly. Something in his voice broke through her haze of self-pity. He almost sounded hurt.

"Nay, I like it here," she said honestly. "'Tis warm and dry and ye are a verra nice mon. But I doona wish te be a burden te ye. Ye have yer own life."

Isobeille ignored the pang of regret that sliced through her, feeling somewhat ashamed for coveting more when she had already been given such a wondrous gift. Nick had a job and a life and had chosen a woman for himself. And as nice as Nick was, she had the distinct impression that her very presence made him uneasy sometimes.

"Let me worry about that, will you? Besides," he said with a wink that had her heart stuttering in her chest, "this is a once-in-a-lifetime opportunity. How many men can say they've gotten the chance to spend time with a six-hundred-plus-year-old Scottish maiden?"

Isobeille smiled but quickly cast her eyes downward lest he see the tears that had begun to pool there. She had spoken the truth, but naught all of it. She had not admitted that leaving was the very last thing she wanted to do. Nor had she revealed that even now, she feared her heart had chosen him as the one it wanted, despite the fact that he belonged to another.

Sharing those insights would serve no favorable purpose. At best, they might make things awkward between them. Isobeille had never felt such an instantaneous and comfortable connection with anyone the way she had with Nick. Ruining that would be even worse than having to face this new world on her own.

At worst, he might come to the same conclusion that her father had – that she was naught but an unwelcome, ungrateful responsibility that he would be glad to get rid of as quickly as possible. Isobeille did not think she could bear it if Nick ever looked at her that way.

With that in mind, she locked those dangerous thoughts deep inside the recesses of her heart and mind. Instead, she would focus on her blessings. She would be grateful for what she had, and would *not* permit the deadly sins of either envy or jealousy to ruin whatever time she had with him. And she would continually remind herself that his desire to have her remain under his protective wing for a while longer was because he was a kind, compassionate, caring man – and not because of requited romantic feelings.

* * *

They finished breakfast and cleaned up together in a companionable silence. Nick was glad for it. After addressing the elephant in the room – namely, Isobeille's immediate future - it was nice to just spend time together, enjoying each other's company and doing ordinary things.

He couldn't help wondering, though, if Isobeille was as relieved as he was that she would be staying with him for a while longer. He *thought* she was, but reading people – especially women – was not his forte. All he had to do was look back at the week before Thanksgiving to remind himself of that.

So instead of trying to figure out what Isobeille was thinking, he opted to focus on what she had actually said. Two things, in particular. One, Isobeille liked it here, and two, she liked *him*. As far as he was concerned, everything else was superfluous.

Beyond that, Nick couldn't help but feel that he had just avoided a major crisis in convincing Isobeille to stay with him a while longer. The question was, why?

Yes, he was genuinely concerned about Isobeille. She might be a grown woman, but in many ways she was like a child – incredibly naïve and knowing very little about her new world. He would have to be a cruel, heartless bastard to turn her out, wouldn't he?

Having her stay for a while – at least until they figured something out – might ease his conscience, but it would create some challenges as well, not the least of which was figuring out how to explain her to his girlfriend.

First things first, though. He needed to find her something else to wear. The dress she had "arrived" in was way too conspicuous, Gloria's stuff didn't fit (at least not well enough to wear in public without inciting a riot), and seeing her in *his* clothes was having some serious side effects that he'd just as soon not think too deeply upon.

Chapter 7

"Yo, Carlos, you have a couple of sisters, right?" Nick held the phone to his ear, smiling to himself as he watched Isobeille try to work his remote, waving it warily at the flat screen as if it might turn around and bite her. She must have seen him turn it on earlier to catch the weather and latest scores.

"Fuck off, man," Carlos said with no little affection. "You might be my partner, but that won't stop me from killing you if you even think about hitting on one of my sisters, no matter how cute they think you are. What, is Gloria cutting you off again?"

Yes, she was, but that seemed the least of his problems at the moment. "Don't be a dick. I need some women's clothes."

"You don't strike me as the cross-dressing type," Carlos chuckled. "You holding out on me, bro?"

"Fuck you. I'm just… helping somebody out."

Carlos was quiet for a moment. Nick knew he was connecting the dots. They'd been partners long enough for Carlos to know Nick's penchant for helping others. He'd often commented that Nick had a heart the size of Texas, though it wasn't always spoken as a compliment.

"Please tell me she's legal."

Considering the fact that Isobeille had been born somewhere around 1390, Nick figured that qualified as legal.

"Yeah, man. And at the risk of repeating myself, fuck you. You going to help me out or not?"

Carlos answered with a long suffering sigh. Though he wouldn't openly admit it, he was every bit as much of a sucker for a damsel in distress as Nick was. It was one of the many reasons they'd hit it off so well from day one.

"Alright, bro. What do you need?"

"Clothes."

"Yeah, got that, fidiot. What *size* do you need?"

"How the hell should I know?" Nick muttered. "Um, hang on a sec." Holding the phone against his chest, he poked his head into the living room where Isobeille was now making complicated geometrical patterns in the air with the remote. She looked like she was casting a spell.

"Do you have any idea what size you are?"

She looked at him for a moment, then used her hands to indicate rectangular dimensions of her approximate height and width.

"No, of course you don't," Nick mumbled

under his breath.

"Holy shit. She's there? At your place?" Carlos yelled into the phone. "Are you insane?"

Nick ignored Carlos' well-meant but totally irrelevant remarks and cut into his tirade. "Hang on, dude. I have to put the phone down for a minute."

"Come here," he commanded Isobeille. Without hesitation, without question, she immediately dropped the remote and came to stand in front of him (a fact that amazed him). The top of her head just barely reached his shoulders, so he figured that put her around five-two or so. He tugged her toward the bathroom, had her step on the scale, leaning over her shoulder to see the digital display. Then he used his forty-inch leather belt to get approximate measurements. Throughout the whole ordeal, she remained silent and cooperative, though she did watch everything he did with great interest.

"Carlos," Nick said, picking up the phone and the remote at the same time. He gave the remote back to Isobeille and pointed at the power button. She tapped it with her finger, her face lighting up with the radiance of the sun when the television came to life.

"About five-two, one-ten. Thirty-eight, twenty-three, thirty-eight." Nick turned away and spoke into the phone. He was met with silence. "Carlos? You still there, man?"

"Are you kidding me?" his partner asked in disbelief.

"No. Just do this for me, please? There's no one else I can ask."

Carlos must have heard the desperation in his voice. "Yeah, man, I got your back. Give me a couple of hours."

"Thanks, man. I owe you."

"Shit yeah, you do, and I'm going to - " Nick disconnected the call without hearing the rest of what Carlos was going to do and walked back into the living room to Isobeille.

"If you think that's cool," he said, pointing to the remote, "wait till I show you Xbox…"

"You're not going to invite me in?" Carlos drawled as Nick took the gym bag from him and attempted to shut the door. His size fourteen, steel-toed work boot prevented it from closing entirely.

"No."

Carlos grinned, his perfect white teeth glistening. "Thirty-eight, twenty-three, thirty-eight? *Really?* You know I'm not leaving till I meet her."

"I really hate you sometimes."

"You love me like a brother."

"I could just shoot you. Hide the body. Nobody'd have to know."

"But you won't, 'cause then there won't be anyone to cover your ugly ass when you mess up."

In general, Nick was a pretty stubborn guy, but he knew his partner was as well. There was little chance this was going to end well, and despite the verbal abuse, Carlos was like a brother to Nick. A brother and a best friend, even if he was an annoying pain in the ass sometimes. There was no one he trusted more.

Nick gave a martyred sigh and stepped back enough to allow the other man to enter.

"Nick!" Isobeille cried excitedly from the other room, waving the controller when she saw him thru the archway. "I have vanquished the evil one!"

He smiled indulgently at her like a star student. "Good job!"

She gave him a huge smile and a hand gesture as Carlos leaned in to get a better look.

"Why is she flipping you off?"

Nick chuckled. "She keeps getting that confused with a 'thumbs-up'."

At the sight of Carlos, Isobeille dropped the controller, and stood, taking a step back. The smile that had filled the room with sunshine only moments earlier was now noticeably absent.

"It's okay, Isobeille," Nick said soothingly. "Carlos is my friend. He brought some clothes for you."

Nick held the bag out to her, but she didn't move. He looked over to find Carlos staring at her intently and thumped him soundly on the back of the head. "Knock it off, man. You're scaring her."

Carlos shook himself free. "Sorry."

Nick gave Isobeille the bag and suggested she change. Only once she was safely behind his bedroom door did Nick turn to Carlos and punch him hard in the arm. "What was that all about?"

"She's..." Carlos seemed at a loss for words.

"Yeah, I know, right? But she's - "

"*Dude. She's the chick from the video.*"

"What the hell are you talking about?"

"You better fire up your Galaxy, man."

Several minutes later, Nick was staring openmouthed as images of Isobeille getting tackled filled the screen of his smartphone.

"I should have known that was you. Who else would be stupid enough to jump in front of a frigging bus? And look at that ugly-ass hair. You really need a haircut, dude."

"Where did this come from?"

Carlos shrugged. "Everyone's got a smartphone now, don't they? My guess is some tourist was just jacking around, got lucky."

Nick replayed the video. It began with a simple, panning view of the busy streets, crowds, and lighted shops. Then there was a flash and a scream, and the view swung around. The clip showed Isobeille in front of the bus, looking terrified as she put up her hands to shield her face. Then a man came out of nowhere and with a running tackle got her out of the way just before both of them were flattened. Nick paled; he hadn't realized just how close she – and he – had actually come to being roadkill.

He winced as he watched them hit – Isobeille taking the brunt of it on her small body. Only the back of him was visible, but there was no mistaking Isobeille's hair and unusual dress.

Those images were closely followed by ones of her on the sidewalk, a close up of her face over his shoulder as she held her hand up to her rescuer's, of the look in her eyes, the wonder. Christ, how had he missed that? No woman had ever looked at him like that. Then again, he was too busy being annoyed with her at the time to notice.

"My sisters were going nuts over it, and they're not the only ones. It's gone viral, bro. Everyone wants to know who she is. Who *you* are."

"Why?"

"Jesus. Are you not looking at the same thing I am? It's like a scene from a chick flick. Man saves beautiful woman, then she looks at him like *that*? You've got every woman sighing from here to the West Coast."

Nick had seen Isobeille in her peasant dress, in Gloria's too-tight clothing, and his workout gear. Therefore he was somewhat prepared and had a chance to steel himself for Isobeille's emergence from his bedroom in her new clothes. Carlos, however, was not as fortunate.

"Damn."

Isobeille stood just outside the kitchen area. In soft faded denims and an even softer white sweater, she looked ... incredible.

"Isobeille," Nick said, rising and going to her. "You look beautiful. Do they fit well?"

"Aye, they do. Thank ye," she said with a shy smile, looking first at Nick and then more warily at Carlos.

"Come on over and meet Carlos. He's ugly, but he doesn't bite. Isobeille, Carlos. Carlos, Isobeille."

"Isobeille," Carlos murmured, looking at her like a lovesick puppy. "A beautiful name for a beautiful woman." He took her hand in his and kissed it, making her blush. Nick rolled his eyes and slapped Carlos' hand away.

"Knock it off, Casanova. She's not interested."

"'Tis a pleasure te meet ye, Carlos," Isobeille said with a slight curtsy.

"You have a lovely accent, Isobeille."

"Isobeille is from Scotland," Nick said quickly.

Carlos grinned widely. "Obviously. What brings you to our fair city, Isobeille?"

"Fate." She glanced at Nick and he chuckled as they shared their private joke. "Give us a minute, will you, Isobeille?"

She nodded, and left them alone.

"Fuck, Nick. I mean, *fuck*."

"Yeah, that pretty much covers it."

"She in some kind of trouble?"

"Isobeille lost everything," Nick said carefully, his tone subtly warning Carlos not to ask too many questions. "I'm just... helping her out a little, that's all."

Carlos shook his head in disbelief. "Does Gloria know?"

"No, not yet," Nick grimaced. "She's been busy."

"You are going to tell her though, right?"

"Yeah, of course."

"I know your heart's in the right place, man, but do you really think this is a good idea?"

Nick shrugged. "Probably not. But I can't just toss her out into the street."

"They've got places that deal with situations like this, people like her."

Nick was shaking his head. "No, not like Isobeille. Trust me on this one, dude."

Carlos grinned. "She can stay with me."

"*So* not happening, bro."

Carlos chuckled, then grew serious. "Seriously, Nick. You sure you're not in over your head on this one?"

"No," Nick answered honestly.

Carlos studied him for a few minutes. "Fair enough. You're a big boy, and one lucky bastard, if you ask me. You need anything, you just ask, yeah?"

"Yeah, thanks," Nick answered, relieved, then

immediately thought of something. "Hey, there is one thing. Your sister still work over at the University?"

"Yeah."

Nick dug into his pocket and pulled out the coin Isobeille had given him. He had thought about showing it to Gloria and asking her to have someone look at it, but this might work out better. He had no idea how Gloria was going to react when she found out about Isobeille, but his instincts told him she wouldn't exactly be thrilled. She was forever telling Nick he was too soft-hearted, that he let people take advantage of his decent nature.

"Ask her to show this to one of the medieval studies profs, get his take on it, maybe find out what something like this is worth. But keep it quiet, okay?

"Sure." Carlos rose to go, stuffing the coin into his pocket. "And hey, if you want me to babysit for a couple of hours, I'm there for you, you know?"

Chapter 8

"Would you like to go for a walk?" Nick asked. He'd been standing in the doorway, watching Isobeille stare out the window. She seemed to do that a lot, as if she was trying to make sense of it all. He could only imagine what it would be like to look out onto the world and not recognize anything. He might not have all the answers, but maybe he could at least help her acclimate to the twenty-first century.

"Could we?" she asked, a spark of interest igniting in her pretty green eyes. He loved seeing her face light up like that; she was so easy to please.

"Sure," he grinned. She had braided her hair. Dressed in a hoodie and jeans, she wouldn't draw too much attention. Now that he knew about the video, he would be careful of taking her out in public – at least until they had a better plan.

Nick held on to her hand. He told himself it was only for her safety, to keep her from walking into things or wandering off, but even he knew it was a lie. He liked holding her hand, feeling the warmth it gave him and the pleasant tingles that radiated up his arm and into the rest of him. He smiled, remembering the first time he had held a girl's hand - Constance McCreary, at recess in the third grade. It had felt kind of like that then, too. And this time their crotchety old teacher, Mrs. Lewinski, wasn't there to put a stop to it.

They walked up one side of the street a couple of blocks, then down the other. Nick didn't think anything of it – he'd walked this path a million times, had long ago stopped noticing the buildings or the shops or the people, but Isobeille's curiosity and excitement was contagious. She was enthralled by the smallest things and asked a million questions, many of which Nick found he couldn't answer (why hadn't he paid more attention in science class?). By the time they stopped near the park, he couldn't seem to wipe the silly-assed grin from his face.

Mentally, he was making a list of all the things he wanted to show her, all the things he had begun taking for granted. It would take weeks, at least.

"Thank ye, Nick," Isobeille said when they made it back to his place. "I had a wonderful day."

"I did, too," he said honestly. They really hadn't done much of anything besides walk around and look at things. He'd spent a grand total of less than ten dollars (roasted peanuts from a street vendor and a Snickers from a Duane Reade), but Isobeille acted as if he had given her the moon.

He waited until Isobeille went into the shower before listening to his voicemail. *Shit*, he cursed softly when he saw the missed call and vmail icons. There was a message from Gloria. He'd completely forgotten that he'd said he'd call her.

He listened to the message, then quickly tapped the call-back icon.

"Hey," he said, when Gloria picked up on the second ring. "Got your message. What's up?"

"I called hours ago."

"Been busy," he said, trying to dispel the image of a naked, wet Isobeille in his bathroom at that very moment. "Get your article done?"

"Mostly. Busy doing what? Didn't you have the day off?"

"Stuff."

He loved being near Isobeille after her shower, when her skin was still dewy and especially fragrant, her long hair twisting into all those curls…

"Does it have anything to do with the redhead you body-slammed on 15th Street last night?"

Nick's thoughts rocketed back into focus at her words. He briefly considered playing the dumb card, but really saw no point. Gloria had recognized him, and he'd been meaning to tell her anyway. It was as good an opening as any.

"Saw that, huh?"

"Who didn't?" She paused, waiting for Nick to say something else. He didn't.

"I knew it was you. Who else would throw himself in front of a bus for someone he's never met?"

"You say it like it's a bad thing," Nick muttered.

"It's all anyone's talking about around the paper," Gloria fished, waiting expectantly for more information.

"It was a spur of the moment thing," he said, opting for partial truth. "I was running late for our date, so I took off after making sure she was okay."

He failed to mention that he turned around right afterward and that she'd been staying with him ever since, wondering why he was so reluctant to tell her those things. Gloria was his girlfriend, after all.

A girlfriend who'd told him she needed to 'find herself' when he last saw her three weeks ago.

"You didn't tell anyone it was me, did you?" he asked, suddenly imagining a bunch of media jackals camping outside his apartment building. He hadn't spotted any when they'd been out earlier, but that could change in a heartbeat if they smelled a story.

"No. But the paper would love to get a scoop on that," she said. "I could write it myself, do an exclusive."

"No," he said, a little too harshly, then added quickly, "Really, there's nothing to tell." Nothing that wouldn't get Isobelle locked up somewhere for observation, anyway, and get his puss in the news, neither of which was a good thing.

"Oh." Gloria somehow managed to convey so much disappointment into that one word that he almost reconsidered. Then her voice changed significantly, dropping into a much more sensual tone. "Listen, how about I come over tonight? We can open up a bottle of wine, light a few candles, talk about you being a big, strong hero."

What?! "Not tonight," Nick heard himself saying, surprising himself. "I'm beat, and I pulled the early shift tomorrow."

Gloria was silent for several long moments. "All right. Call me tomorrow?"

"Yeah, sure."

Nick put down the phone and stared at it as if it might bite him. What had he just done? Then he heard Isobeille singing, and thought about snuggling on the couch again with her, maybe ordering some Chinese and watching some corny animated Christmas classics, and everything else just kind of faded into the background…

"You know how to work the TV and Blu-Ray. There's a stack of DVDs over there. Feel free to watch whatever you want, but most are probably a bit on the violent side."

"Thank ye."

"We can go shopping later, but there should be enough food for you. There's soup and crackers and a couple of frozen boxed things in the freezer. You're okay working the can opener and the microwave, right?"

He'd explained and demonstrated both the night before.

"Aye."

"Don't leave the apartment, okay? We'll go out when I get back if you want, but you shouldn't be wandering around by yourself. You might get lost, and there's all kinds of nut sacks out there."

She smiled serenely, her hands clasped in front of her.

"If you need anything, just go next door to Mrs. Anderson. She's a real nice lady. She knows you're here – not any of the details, of course – but she may stop by later just to say hi and see how you're doing. But don't open the door for anyone else, got it?"

Isobeille nodded somberly. "Got it."

"I'll call if I get a break. Don't pick up unless you hear my name on the machine. If there's an emergency, or something happens, go next door to Mrs. Anderson's and call me from there; she has my work and cell numbers. She'll know what to do."

"All right."

Christ, he felt like shit leaving her alone like this. He walked toward the door, got as far as putting his hand on the knob, then turned around.

"Maybe I should just call in today. I can get someone else to cover my shift. God knows I covered for them often enough."

"Nick," Isobeille said softly, laying her hand on his arm. "I will be fine. Go. Save people."

He still looked doubtful, so she raised up on her toes to place a chaste kiss on his cheek. "*Go*. And I will be waiting for ye, hale and hearty, when ye return."

"Promise?" he said, unable to help himself.

"Aye," she smiled shyly. "I promise."

Cheek still tingling, he forced his feet to carry him out the door.

Chapter 9

The morning passed quickly; he and Carlos were called out several times. As it got closer to Christmas, more and more people were heading into the city, which meant more accidents, more injuries, more heart attacks from the stress of it all. Thankfully, most of them weren't life-threatening, but it certainly made for a busy shift. It was past noon when he finally got the chance to call Isobeille.

He held his breath, counting the four rings until his machine picked up. So far, so good; Isobeille was doing exactly as he told her. It made him worry a little less, in any event.

"Isobeille, it's Nick. It's okay to pick up the phone."

Back at his apartment, Isobeille dutifully removed the handset from the base unit.

"Isobeille?"

"Yes?" she spoke, looking toward the unit.

"Isobeille, you can pick up the handset. It's Nick."

"I did. 'Tis in my hand right now," she said, yelling a bit. Mayhap you had to talk especially loud into these things to be heard, she reasoned.

A few moments of silence ticked by, then Nick chuckled as he realized what was probably happening. "Isobeille, press the green button on the left of the handset." She quickly located said button and did as instructed.

"NICK!" she yelled.

Nick held the phone away from his ear and laughed. "You don't need to yell. Just talk normally and I'll hear you."

"Oh, my apologies."

He was so glad he called; just hearing her voice was already improving his mood.

"No problem. My bad – I should have shown you how to use it." He took modern technology for granted; it was easy to forget that this was all new to her.

"Is everything going okay?"

"Oh, aye," she said, and he could picture her smiling. "I took a verra long shower. I hope ye doona mind. I must say, 'tis so far my most favorite thing of yer time." She was quick to add, "Weel, besides ye, of course."

He grinned, ignoring the little tug in his gut that was becoming as common as the tightness in his groin. "Surely you didn't spend the entire morning in the shower?"

"Nay," she said, with a light laugh that made him wish he was there so he could see her eyes sparkling, too. "Yer neighbor stopped by. Did ye know she was of Scottish ancestry? She invited me over for coffee. Can I go?"

The idea made him nervous; he was feeling quite protective of Isobeille, but she sounded so excited that he didn't have the heart to say no. Besides, Mrs. Anderson was a really sweet lady. Isobeille would be safe with her.

"No, I didn't know that. Of course you can go over to her place for coffee. Just... be careful. Mrs. Anderson is a nice lady, but she's a woman and a mother, which means she's nosy by nature and will probably ask you lots of questions." Like where she came from and how she met Nick. "Best to keep to our little story, I think."

"Doona fash. I ken how te keep a wee secret or twa, aye?"

The silly-assed grin was still on his face several minutes after he disconnected the call. He loved the way she talked to him, the things that she said. Four hours left in his shift, and he was already anxious to get home. It was an unfamiliar feeling, but then, he usually didn't have much to go home to, either.

"Isobeille is still at your place, I take it?" Carlos guessed when Nick rejoined him in the truck to head out for their next call. Nick had been edgy all morning, but after one mysterious phone call he was grinning like an idiot. It wasn't exactly rocket science. There was only one thing that could adjust a man's attitude that quickly, and in Nick's case, it came in the form of a curvy little redhead with big green eyes and a smile that could light up the city at night.

"Yeah." That one word and the smile that went with it said it all.

Carlos grinned. He *knew* it. He just wondered when Nick would figure it out.

Nick almost turned around and walked back out to re-check the number on the apartment door. He *thought* he was going into his place, but something didn't seem right. The moment he opened the door, he walked into comfortable warmth, soft light, and the most delicious aromas.

"Isobeille?"

He found her in the kitchen, stirring something in a big pot on top of the stove. "Isobeille?"

She turned and saw him, the smile on her face setting off a series of little explosions in his chest.

"Nick! Ye are home!"

He rubbed absently at the center of his torso. There was something about seeing her there in his kitchen, so pleased to see him that was making him feel like he just sucked in sunlight.

"What are you doing?"

"Ah, weel, I got te thinking 'twould be nice te have something for ye when ye got home."

"You cooked?" The last time Nick had a

home-cooked meal – one he hadn't made himself – was when he went back to his mom's for Thanksgiving a few weeks earlier. He couldn't remember when the last time was before that.

"Aye."

"But where did you get all this?"

"That cold box right there," she said, pointing at the refrigerator. "I hope ye doona mind."

Nick had forgotten the frozen packages of stuff his mom had sent him home with. Twenty-eight years old and his mom was still giving him care packages like he was in college. Not that he minded. It was nice to have someone who cared enough to do so.

"Are you kidding?" he said, his stomach growling in anticipation. "It smells fantastic."

Nick took what had to be one of the quickest showers in history, then changed into his most comfortable jeans and pull-over. Re-entering the small kitchen area, he glanced around at the variety of dishes she had prepared, at the table settings, the candles. He had candles?

"All this was really in my kitchen?" he asked incredulously. It seemed hard to fathom.

"Aye."

"You figured out how to work the stove alright, obviously."

"It wasnae so difficult," she said, spooning a ladle of something heavenly into a bowl before him. She was serving him, too? His inner caveman – the one he had only recently discovered – grunted in appreciation.

"'Tis a lot harder te cook over a fire, ye ken. Ye doona have the same control. And I did have a wee bit of help - Mrs. Anderson seemed verra glad te show me."

That first bite melted in his mouth, so good that Nick closed his eyes to savor it. "This is fantastic, Isobeille."

She blushed and averted her eyes, which he thought was adorably sweet, but she was obviously pleased. That made two of them. He hadn't realized how nice it could be to come home after a long, hard day and share a meal with someone. It was something a guy could get used to pretty easily. No wonder his dad always made it a priority to be home from work in time for dinner.

"I hope you weren't too bored today," he said in between mouthfuls. Damn, she was a good cook.

"Bored? Nay," she shook her head. "I had plenty te keep me busy, and Mrs. Anderson is a lovely woman, verra kind."

"Did she ask you lots of questions?"

"Och, aye, but doona fash. I dinnae lie, but I was careful aboot what I said. I told her that ye were verra kindly letting me stay with ye for a wee bit. She took it upon herself te fill in some of the details; I saw no reason te contradict her."

When Nick raised an eyebrow in question, she shrugged and added. "Weel, it would have been verra rude."

Before he could ask exactly what those "details" entailed, Isobeille said, "I would much rather hear about yer day. Tell me, Nick Peterson, of yer brave and noble deeds this day."

Nick felt the color rise in his cheeks again. If it had been anyone else besides Isobeille uttering such words he would have felt certain they were mocking him, but one look into her big green eyes and he knew she meant every word of it.

And so, over the delicious meal, he told her all about the calls he and Carlos had made. About the multi-car pileup on the interstate. The drive-by downtown that left a fourteen-year-old innocent bystander fighting for his life. The woman who ended up delivering twins in the back of a taxi stuck in gridlock.

Throughout it all, Isobeille listened with rapt attention, asking questions and praising all the good that he and Carlos had done, the positive differences they'd made in so many lives. It was good for his ego. By the time he'd eaten his fill, he could almost believe he was at least partially the hero she made him out to be.

As they put the leftovers away – Isobeille had made enough to feed several hungry men, Nick had had enough of talking about himself. As nice as it was, it felt strange; usually he was the one listening to someone else, not the other way around. Nick wasn't comfortable talking about himself or his job, but Isobeille made it so easy. She was an excellent listener, and seemed genuinely interested in what he had to say.

It was different. And... nice.

"Hey," he said, as they put the last of the dishes away. "How'd you like to get out of this box for a little while? There's something I'd like to show you tonight, if you're up for it."

That quickly, her eyes lit up with excitement, and Nick found himself grinning as well.

Outside it was cold, but not unpleasant, especially with Isobeille's hand tucked neatly into his. Like before, he told himself it was only to keep her from stumbling or wandering off, but that excuse was wearing thin. If he was honest with himself, he'd have to admit that he just plain liked the feel of her hand in his. It made him feel good, he was discovering, like so many things about her.

It took a bit longer than expected to make it down to the square. Isobeille was easily distracted, pausing to admire window displays and decorations every few feet. Nick didn't mind so much, though. Watching Isobeille, seeing her joy, sharing her sense of excitement and discovery, made it worthwhile.

About half a block from their final destination, Nick made Isobeille close her eyes. He led her up to the square, then positioned her very carefully before telling her to open them again.

Isobeille popped her eyes open and

immediately gasped. Before them stood a fifty-foot spruce lit with thousands of tiny lights and adorned with shiny glistening ornaments and shimmery ribbons.

"Oh, Nick," she breathed, taking in the scene before her. "'Tis the most glorious thing I have ever seen! What do ye call it?"

"A Christmas tree," he answered, smiling back at her. "Don't you celebrate Christmas?"

"Och, aye. 'Tis a time of great celebration and Holiness. I have heard of a few lairds having small evergreens placed in the Great Halls amidst the feasts, but more often 'twas boughs of holly adorning the door. Nothing like this, ye ken. 'Tis enormous! Like the trees in the ancient forest!"

"Tell me more about Christmas in your time," Nick prompted, slipping his hand over hers again. It was the first time he had asked her to share anything about her prior life since the night of her arrival, and hoped he was not making a mistake in bringing up her past.

"Weel, some things are the same, I think," she said after a moment or two of consideration. "The womenfolk spend days baking, like yer neighbor, but instead of cookies they make Black Buns and Sun Cakes."

"Black Buns and Sun Cakes?"

"Aye. The more modern families make the Black Buns or the Twelfth Night Cakes. 'Tis a verra rich cake, quite solid, with fruit, almonds, spices, and copious amounts of whiskey," she grinned. "The ones who follow the ancient ways prefer Sun Cakes. They are baked with a hole in the center and lines around like the rays of the sun."

"Which do you prefer?" he asked.

"I made both," she told him with a twinkle in her eye. "Albeit, the Sun Cakes were more popular. 'Twas common te receive the Black Buns as weel-meant gifts, but most became treats for the goats, ye ken."

Nick laughed too, telling Isobeille about the similar stigma of fruitcakes in the modern world.

"We doona have lights like ye do," she continued as they walked along, hand in hand, "but on Christmas Eve, one and all would light candles in the windows to welcome and draw a stranger or twa. 'Twas called *Oidche Choinnle*, or the Night of Candles."

Applying modern thinking to the ancient tradition, Nick couldn't imagine openly inviting strangers into a home like that, not even in the quiet, rural community in which he was raised, let alone the city (present company excluded, of course). "Sounds dangerous. Why would you do that?"

"By honoring the visit of a stranger inte yer home that night, ye honor the Holy Family, who searched for shelter the night of the Christ child's birth."

When she said it like that, he felt a little ashamed, though Nick sincerely doubted they had the kind of crime rate in medieval Scotland that was so prevalent today.

"And most of the menfolk had really big swords," she added with a wry grin. "Only a fool would even think te enter another mon's home with a foul purpose on such a holy night."

Isobeille looped her arm through Nick's as they ventured further about the square, checking out the other decorations. He didn't even think about stopping her; it felt far too good to have her on his arm.

"The biggest celebration comes after Christmas, though," Isobeille continued. "Hogmanay, ye ken. Four days of reverie to mark the New Year. There's the Redding of the House, and First Footing, of course. Then there's the Fire Festivals and group Sing-A-Longs. 'Tis all very festive."

She turned to find Nick grinning at her. "What?"

"Your eyes. They light up like that Christmas tree when something excites or pleases you."

She lowered her eyes and blushed, and Nick felt warmth spread through him like good liquor.

"Hey. Don't be embarrassed."

"'Tis just... ye say the loveliest things. I dinnae expect ye te have such a honeyed tongue."

Honeyed tongue? Him? He had never been good at saying the right thing when it came to women. It was one of the reasons he let them do most of the talking. But with Isobeille, it was so easy. He didn't even have to think about what to say; it just kind of came out on its own.

Then again, it seemed everything was different with Isobeille.

Nick was deep in those thoughts when he felt Isobeille slowing beside him, her gaze locked upon something deep in the shadows of the alley. Nick tightened his grip on her protectively; after living in the city for several years, Nick knew that it was best to keep his eyes to the front and his feet moving forward past such areas, but he hadn't had a chance to teach Isobeille those kind of urban survival skills yet.

"Isobeille," he warned quietly. "Come on."

She obeyed, but slowed again once they had taken several steps past the alleyway. "What was that mon doing?" she asked.

Nick didn't have to ask what man she was referring to. He had followed her gaze to the dark figure huddled in the corner carefully arranging flattened pieces of corrugated cardboard.

"He's probably homeless," Nick said, his voice holding none of the mirth it had only minutes before.

"Homeless? Ye mean he has nowhere te live?"

Nick shook his head. "Probably not. It happens. People lose their jobs, have a turn of bad luck, find themselves out on the streets. Then there are those who lose everything because of things like drugs and alcohol."

Isobeille frowned, no doubt thinking of her own father. "He has no kin? Nowhere te go?"

Nick shrugged, uncomfortable with the empathy he saw in Isobeille's eyes. "Who knows? It's different for everyone. But the city does have shelters where people can go when it gets too cold or when they need a hot meal."

"Like the ones ye told me aboot," she frowned.

"Yeah. But sometimes the shelters are even worse than the streets. And some people are too proud to ask for help. They'd rather tough it out on their own."

Isobeille was quiet for a few minutes. "There must be something we can do, Nick."

He studied her face, saw the determination and hope in her expression, and exhaled heavily. "Yeah, you're right. Come on."

An hour later, Nick and Isobeille walked out of the alley. The man she had seen earlier now had a blanket, three pairs of socks, a scarf, a pair of Nick's old boots, a thermos of Isobeille's stew and fifty bucks. For as long as he lived, Nick would never forget the look on the man's face when they showed up with the box of stuff, or the way he had grasped Isobeille's hand and called her an angel of the Lord.

It seemed that, in meeting Isobeille, Nick had finally met someone who was an even bigger sucker than he was. The thought warmed his heart.

"Come on," he said, tucking her a little closer. "I know this place that has the best hot chocolate…"

Chapter 10

Things quickly settled into a comfortable routine. Each morning Isobeille would rise at the same time he did and prepare him a hot breakfast (she really got the hang of the kitchen quite quickly). While Nick was working, Isobeille found plenty to keep herself busy. She cleaned and tidied Nick's apartment – something Nick repeatedly asked her not to do. It was the only time Isobeille did not acquiesce, insisting that it was the very least she could do since he was providing her with food and shelter until they figured out something else. In truth, neither of them was trying really hard to make progress on that front.

For at least an hour each afternoon, Isobeille would have coffee with Mrs. Anderson. The two women seemed to take to each other immediately, and for that, Nick was glad. In his older neighbor, Isobeille had found a friend and someone who was happy to share all kinds of information with her. Even more important to him, Nick felt much better about leaving Isobeille during the day, knowing that Mrs. Anderson was there and keeping an eye on her.

During those times when she was not cleaning, cooking, or spending time with Mrs. Anderson, Isobeille dedicated her time to the discovery of new things. Nick showed her how to use his laptop and introduced her to the wonders of Google and Wikipedia. Isobeille was a fast learner; she picked up the use of digital technology very quickly. She happily spent many hours exploring, awed by the sheer amount of knowledge available instantly at her fingertips. Curious by nature, she often lost herself for hours in the virtual world.

When Nick came home in the evening to a wonderful meal, she would tell him all that she had learned that day, and he would share his day as well. They would clean up the kitchen together, then spend their evenings walking around the city, watching a movie, or just talking.

He loved it all, but Nick's favorite time of day was when they cuddled up together on the couch and Isobeille would fall asleep in his arms. He didn't think he'd ever felt as content as he did in those moments.

"Nick." The familiar voice shocked him out of his reverie as he lifted the phone to his ear.

"Gloria."

"Is everything alright?" she asked, sounding a bit worried. He wasn't used to hearing concern in her voice.

"Yeah. Why wouldn't it be?"

"You haven't called once all week."

A week? Really? Had it been that long? It seemed like the days were just flying by.

"Yeah, well. You said you needed space, right?" he said, remembering the last time they'd hooked up. They'd been seeing each other for six months, and in his mind, at least, things had been going well enough to proceed to the next step - introducing her to the family. Gloria, however, had balked at the idea. She'd declined, saying she wasn't ready to take things to a "meet-the-parent" level. At the time, Nick told her that he understood, but it had hurt more than he'd let on.

"You're still mad about that?" she asked.

"No," he said honestly. "I'm not mad."

At the time he'd been hurt, and maybe a little angry, but oddly enough, that seemed to have faded since then. Of course, he had a lot of other things occupying his attention lately and hadn't had the time – or the inclination - to dwell on it.

"Then why are you being like this?"

"Being like what?" he asked a bit sharply, a hint of frustration edging into his voice. "Giving you what you wanted?"

Gloria was quiet for a minute. "I'm sorry, Nick. You're right."

It was Nick's turn to grow silent. He'd never heard either of those phrases from Gloria's lips before, much less both in the same breath. It seemed contrary to her nature, actually.

"Nick? Are you still there?"

"Yeah."

"So, I was thinking I'd come over tonight and we could… do something."

Nick looked into the living room where Isobeille was making intricate little bows with some shiny iridescent ribbon she'd found at the Dollar Store for his tiny little tree. They'd covered it with a couple of sets of miniature twinkling, multi-colored lights. At that moment she turned and smiled at him, a smile filled with such genuine happiness that he felt it all the way into the pit of his stomach.

"Sorry, Gloria. I can't tonight."

"Oh." Another awkward silence stretched between them. "We are still on for the Christmas party tomorrow night, though, right?"

Nick gripped the phone harder. He had forgotten all about that. She'd told him about it weeks ago – the annual party the newspaper threw for its employees, no expense spared. It was, according the Gloria, *the* most important event of the year, and one that anybody who hoped to become *somebody* at the paper did not miss.

"Yeah, of course," he said without thinking.

"Great. Pick me up at eight?"

"Eight. Yep. Got it." *Shit*. How did he get himself into this? He should have just told her that something had come up, because really, it was the truth...

"Nick?"

"Yeah?"

"I'm really looking forward to seeing you. I... miss you."

"Yeah, uh, me, too," Nick mumbled in return, then hung up and scrubbed his hand over his face. How could he have forgotten about the Christmas party? How could he have forgotten about *Gloria*?

He wasn't sure how long he stood there before he felt Isobeille's soft touch. "Nick? Is everything alright? Ye look vexed."

He looked into her eyes, suddenly feeling incredibly guilty. "Yeah, everything's fine. It's just, well, I forgot that I said I'd go to this party tomorrow. It's not really something I can bail on last minute, either. It was before you came, otherwise I never would have agreed."

"Nick," she scolded gently. "Ye arenae worried about leaving me here alone, are ye?"

"Kind of," he admitted, feeling like a first-class idiot. Mostly he just didn't want to go, preferring to spend the evening with Isobeille. "I mean, I know you're here all day by yourself, but nights are different."

Evenings were *their* time, and he was loath to give up even a single one.

She laughed, the sound like quiet musical bells. "Ye are a verra sweet mon, but doona worry. Ye spend all yer time working and looking after me. Ye need some time te have fun."

"I have fun with you."

What Isobeille didn't seem to realize was that "looking after her" as she so put it *was* fun – more fun than he'd had in a very long time. He liked spending time with her. Isobeille found wonder in the smallest of things, and it made him appreciate them, too. It was like he was rediscovering everything, looking at things in a whole new light. Even more than that, Nick felt like a different man when he was with Isobeille. Younger. Happier. *Better*.

"Hey man," Carlos said after Nick repacked the same supply kit for the third time. "Where's your head today? It's like you are a million miles away."

"Sorry. I've just got a lot on my mind."

Carlos handed a cup of coffee to Nick and sat down next to him, his legs hanging off the back of their rig. "Wouldn't happen to have anything to do with a certain curvy little redhead now, would it?"

"No. Yes. *Fuck*." It wasn't *all* about Isobeille specifically, but she was at the center of it, the source of all his fucked-up feelings. He used to think he knew exactly what he wanted, but now he wasn't so sure. Ever since Isobeille came into his life, nothing seemed the same.

"Well, I guess that clears that up," Carlos smirked. "Are you sleeping with her?"

"No! Christ, no." *She makes special meals just for me. Her eyes light up the second I walk in the room. And every night she falls asleep in my arms. But we are most definitely not having sex.* If they were, he wouldn't be taking cold showers every day and running low on lotion.

"Maybe you should. You know you want to. She is smoking hot, dude." Carlos shook his head. "Honestly? I don't know how you're *not* tapping that. If she was staying at my place, looking at me the way she looks at you, I'd be on her like white on rice, bro."

Nick bristled. He didn't like Carlos talking about Isobeille that way, as if she was nothing more than a convenient lay. If he tried really hard, he might even convince himself he didn't want to spend the next three days buried deep inside her lush, warm body.

"Quit thinking with your dick all the time, man. Isobeille's not like that."

"*All* girls are like that," Carlos disagreed. "Some are just more discerning than others, but they'll all give it up for the right one. Me, she wouldn't give the time of day. But you? She'd take you in there in a heartbeat, bro."

Would she? Yeah, Nick realized, she probably would. Which is exactly why he couldn't let it happen. Isobeille wasn't the type of woman he could have once and walk away from. No, if he had allowed himself to have sex with Isobeille, he'd be putting a lot more than just his cock into her. And he couldn't do that. He just had to remember *why* he couldn't do that, and that was getting harder and harder to do with each day he spent in her company, especially when she trusted him so completely.

"She makes me see the world differently, you know? And it's making me think that maybe some of the things I thought were important aren't so much anymore."

"By 'things' you mean Gloria?"

"Yeah. Maybe. I don't know." Gloria was a big part of it, but there was so much more to it than that. Like the fact that Isobeille thought being a paramedic was a wonderful thing in itself, not just a stepping stone to something more. Or the fact that she cared enough to help a homeless guy when she could have just ignored him like most people. Or that there was more fun to be had in a cup of hot chocolate and a quiet evening at home instead of some lame party where everyone dressed up and kissed ass while sipping expensive champagne and pretending to actually give a shit.

"Gloria called last night and reminded me about this party I said I'd go to a couple of weeks back. I'd forgotten all about it. I went a whole week without even calling her, man. What do you suppose that means?"

Carlos knew exactly what that meant, but Nick

clearly wasn't ready to hear it yet, so instead of spelling it out, he shrugged. Nick would figure it out eventually. "You going?"

"Yeah," he sighed heavily. "I don't really want to, but it would be kind of a dick move if I bailed on her at the last minute."

"Like she bailed on you for Bubba's picnic? Or Sandy's wedding? Or turned you down flat when you asked her to go with you to your mom's?" Carlos said, ticking the incidents off on his fingers while reminding Nick that Gloria didn't have the same compunction against leaving him hanging.

Nick grunted and held up his hand to stop a list that could conceivably continue on for some time. "Alright, I get the point. But it's exactly because I know how shitty it is to do that to someone that I won't do it to someone else, true?"

Carlos couldn't argue with that. Nick was a decent guy, which was just one of the many reasons why Gloria was so wrong for him and Isobeille was so right. "So what does Isobeille say?"

Nick looked so tortured Carlos genuinely felt for him; the guy had it bad. "She says I should go and have fun. That I spend too much time worrying about her."

"Do you?"

Nick sighed. "Every moment she's out of my sight, man. But when I'm with her? I don't worry about *anything*."

Carlos whistled. "Wow, bro. You do have a problem." They paused, taking the opportunity to drain the last of their crappy cups of coffee. Then they packed up the re-loaded kits, checked the fasteners, and closed the doors. "So what are you going to do?"

"Don't know what else I can do. I'll go to the party. See what happens."

"And Isobeille?"

"She's going to hang out with Mrs. Anderson."

"Your neighbor?"

"Yeah, Isobeille loves her. They're going to bake cookies for Mrs. Anderson's church group or something."

Carlos couldn't resist giving Nick a little nudge in the right direction. "The party's probably going to run late. I could head over there, keep Isobeille company till you get home."

Nick pinned him with a fierce glare. "I like you, man, but I *will* kill you."

Carlos was still laughing as he drove out of the lot.

Chapter 11

Isobeille would never admit it to Nick, but she was worried. Tonight he would be seeing his beloved again, escorting her to some fancy affair. He would spend the evening reveling with her, feasting, dancing, while Isobeille remained behind. She had smiled and told him that he should go, that she wanted him to have a good time and honor the commitment he had made, but mayhap she should not have encouraged him so. The raw truth of it was that the very thought made her slightly ill.

In her heart, she continued to hope that he would change his mind, making a conscious (and uninfluenced) choice to spend the eve with her instead. It was silly, of course. A foolish girl's hope and nothing more.

Over the past week, she had come to care for him deeply. Her mind knew it was wrong, but she could not help the way she felt. From that very first moment, when she had looked into those warm brown eyes, she had begun to fall in love with him, and each moment since her feelings for him had only grown.

She'd tried to tell herself over and over again that it was not meant to be; that Nick had already chosen the woman he wanted for his own. But her heart wouldn't listen. It saw only what it wanted to – the kindness, the generosity, the gentleness of the man who had quite literally saved her life, brought her into his home and had seen to her care and comfort ever since. It did not want to acknowledge that he had done these things purely out of a sense of decency or chivalry, or simply because he was a good and merciful soul.

Instead of admitting the truth, she had done everything she could think of to please him, to show him her gratitude. Now she realized that she had been subconsciously doing so in the hopes that he might see her as not just a woman who needed his charity, but as a potential bride as well. She had done all of the things a woman does for the man she cares for – she cleaned for him, cooked meals for him, listened attentively and cared for him the best she was able.

It had been no great effort on her part, for she had loved every minute of it. Caring for Nick, trying to make him happy, had been one of the easiest and most rewarding things she had ever done.

Because, no matter how many times she had lied to herself about her intentions, it had happened anyway. She was in love with him. Hopelessly, madly in love with him.

She had begun to think that he might have some tender feelings for her, as well. He smiled at her a lot, said lovely things that made her blush. He was appreciative of her efforts and was generous with praise and thanks, even for the smallest of things. He held her hand whenever they ventured out, and seemed to enjoy their chaste cuddling at night before sleep. She had even seen evidence of his masculine interest several times, though he had made no attempt to act upon it.

She wouldn't have stopped him if he had. God forgive her, she had never wanted a man as fiercely as she wanted him. She would gladly give up her maidenhead to experience even one night of passion in his arms...

Isobeille heard the key in the lock and her heart leaped. Nick was home early! Mayhap he had changed his mind about the party! She turned around, excited by the possibility that Nick might be choosing her after all. Her excitement quickly faded, however, when she saw that it was not Nick that stood in the doorway, but a woman who looked every bit as surprised to see Isobeille as Isobeille was to see her.

"Who are you and what are you doing in Nick's apartment?" the stranger demanded.

Isobeille instinctively knew she was looking at Nick's beloved by the way the little hairs on the back of her neck rose like hackles. The woman was tall and slender, with light golden hair the color of a winter sunrise, aristocratic features, and kohl-lined eyes the color of a summer sky. She was bedecked in high-heeled shoes and a long coat of supple-looking dark leather.

With her waist-length braid, sweatpants, T-shirt, and sneakers, Isobeille suddenly felt very plain in comparison.

"I am Isobeille," she answered, remembering her manners and inclining her head slightly. "And I am preparing a meal. May I inquire as te how ye got in here?"

The woman's gaze was as sharp as a finely-honed blade as she looked Isobeille up and down. It was hard not to fidget beneath the force of her stare, but Isobeille had had enough practice dealing with laird's wives and consorts to hold her own. With a potato in one hand and a peeler in the other, she set her shoulders and waited for an answer.

"With my key. The one *Nick* gave me," she answered, emphasizing his name. The woman's eyes left Isobeille and glanced around the apartment. They scanned the gleaming appliances, took in the just-scrubbed floor, and paused briefly on the basket of Nick's freshly laundered-clothes before coming back to rest on Isobeille again. "Are you like a maid or something?"

Outwardly, she kept her expression neutral, but inside, Isobeille's heart fell and her mind raced. Clearly Nick had not mentioned her at all to his beloved, nor had he shared the fact that he was allowing her to stay with him. But what exactly did that mean?

The hopelessly romantic side of her wanted to believe that perhaps Nick viewed her and their time together as special and private, something to be treasured and shared between only the two of them. The realistic side of her – the one that had given her the strength and means to endure – suggested that the truth was far less appealing. Perhaps Nick was ashamed of her. Perhaps he expected that she would not be around long enough to warrant such disclosure.

Or, she thought, looking at the cold and accusing look in the other woman's eyes, 'twas more likely Nick knew his woman would not take kindly to Isobeille's presence, and had kept his silence so as not to fall into disfavor with his beloved.

At the moment, it mattered not. Nick had been extremely kind to her, providing food and shelter and friendship. He had never promised more than that; any visions she'd had of it becoming something more were of her own creation. He had his reasons, and it was not her place to second-guess them. Despite the ache in her chest, Isobeille would not betray him, nor would she knowingly do anything to cause him angst.

"Nick has been verra kind," she said, choosing her words carefully. "He allows me te clean and cook for him while he is at work."

Gloria stared at her for a minute, then some of the jealousy faded from her Nordic features. "Yeah, that's exactly the kind of thing he would do. He always had a soft spot for strays. Well, sweetheart, today's your lucky day. You get to leave early. I'll take it from here."

Isobeille bit her tongue, silently considering her options. She had the distinct impression that his beloved's arrival was unexpected; surely he would have forewarned her if he had known. What would Nick want her to do?

He was very adamant about keeping to the apartment when he was not around, and reminded her every morning not to open the door for anyone beside Mrs. Anderson. Should she leave, as the woman obviously wanted her to? Or should she remain exactly where she was until Nick returned and sorted things out?

"Don't worry," the woman added, laying the garment bag she carried across the back of the nearest chair. "You won't get into trouble. I'll tell him I told you to leave."

Isobeille couldn't see any graceful way to handle the situation, at least not in a way that wouldn't embarrass Nick or reveal something he obviously did not want revealed – namely, *her*. And, as Nick's chosen, the woman certainly held more authority here than Isobeille did.

"As ye wish." Isobeille turned and began to tidy up the counter.

"Just let that stuff go," the woman said impatiently. "I'll get it later."

Isobeille nodded and grabbed the coat from the peg beside the door, the one Nick had procured for her. It was the nicest covering she had ever had, very pretty, white with green accents that he said brought out her eyes.

"Have a good night, then," Isobeille said.

"Oh, I will," the woman assured her with a grin that showed every one of her straight, pearly white teeth as she closed the door behind Isobeille.

In the corridor, Isobeille leaned against the wall and took a few moments to gather herself together before she walked the short distance to Mrs. Anderson's. She had never met *Gloria* before, but she'd met enough like her. Human nature hadn't changed much in the last six centuries. Even in her village there had been the cold, calculating types who used their beauty to their advantage.

And Gloria *was* beautiful. Her hair was perfectly styled into a short, chic cut; her makeup skillfully applied. She reminded Isobeille of several of the lairds' wives of her own time. And next to her, Isobeille felt every bit like the poor peasant girl she was.

Isobeille took a deep breath and forced a smile to her face before she raised her hand and knocked on Mrs. Anderson's door. It was yet another skill she had learned early on – how to hide her pain from others. One, unfortunately, that she'd had far too much practice to perfect.

"Isobeille, dear!" Mrs. Anderson exclaimed as she opened the door. I wasn't expecting you until later! Come in, come in, dear. Oh, I am so glad you came over early. I was going to call you..."

* * *

Nick was not looking forward to the Christmas party. He hated the thought of putting on a tux (damn, he had to remember to pick that up) and driving all the way uptown to spend the entire evening schmoozing and making inane small talk with the suits while Gloria and every other employee played kiss-the-ass-of-the-execs. Hers was a political job, he got that, and a certain amount of brown-nosing was as much a requirement for the job as a degree in journalism was. But he didn't have to like it.

He would much rather spend the night with Isobeille. Having a nice dinner, cleaning up together. Maybe taking a walk or watching one of those silly Christmas videos she'd taken a liking to.

It didn't help that Carlos' words had been bouncing around in his head all afternoon, either. He couldn't stop thinking about what it would be like to make love to Isobeille; to kiss her and stroke her when they snuggled into the couch. To feel her warm, soft skin naked against his beneath the covers. To bury himself in all that lush, fragrant flesh while she moaned his name in that brogue he loved so much...

Nick shook his head and tried to focus. Those thoughts would definitely *not* help him get through this evening. It had been weeks since he and Gloria last had sex, and his little morning solos in the bathroom weren't doing much to take the edge off anymore. With each day he spent in Isobeille's presence, each night she curled up in his arms, his desire for her grew.

He took a left turn at 3rd Avenue to hit the rental place. On a whim, Nick made a quick stop and picked up a pretty little bouquet of red and white flowers at the flower shop next door. Isobeille would love them. Maybe they would help assuage some of the guilt he felt about going out tonight (and why, exactly, did he feel guilty for taking his girlfriend to a party he'd committed to weeks ago?).

Isobeille hadn't said much about it after telling him he should go. She'd been every bit as pleasant as usual this morning at breakfast, and had actually said she was looking forward to making cookies with Mrs. Anderson. That made him feel a little better. At least Isobeille wouldn't be left alone in his apartment all evening, watching those damn videos all by herself. But he couldn't help the stab of disappointment that she hadn't seemed to mind the fact that he'd be going out with Gloria at all. Even the thought of Isobeille spending time with another man gave him the sensation of talons raking along his insides.

Chapter 12

"Please excuse me for a moment, dear," Mrs. Anderson said when the knock sounded at the door. She returned moments later with a tall, handsome man.

"This is my son, Ian," she said, beaming proudly. "He's a professor at the University. Ian, dear, this is the young lady I was telling you about – Isobeille."

"It's a pleasure to meet you, Isobeille," Ian said, holding out his hand. The auburn-haired man towered over his petite mother, his smile warm and friendly.

Isobeille, who had seen other people greeting each other in this manner, wiped her powdered sugared hands on the apron Mrs. Anderson had lent her and put her hand in his, though she couldn't completely stop the reflexive bow that came naturally with it.

"'Tis a pleasure te meet ye as weel, Mr. Anderson."

He grinned widely. He had a very nice smile, Isobeille thought, one that put her instantly at ease, though it did not make her heart race as Nick's did.

"You weren't kidding, were you?" he chuckled, glancing at his mother, then back at Isobeille. "She told me she'd met a proper Scottish lass, but I must confess, I thought she was pulling my leg."

Isobeille looked down at his leg, bemused, which only made him chuckle more. "I thought she was exaggerating," he clarified.

He had striking blue eyes, Isobeille thought, just like his mother. They radiated intelligence and curiosity, and were clearly visible through the wire-rimmed glasses perched atop his straight nose.

"Ian's taking me out for dinner," Mrs. Anderson explained.

"How lovely for ye," Isobeille said sincerely. "I can get the rest of these out of the oven if ye wish te get yerself ready."

The older woman thanked Isobeille and did just that, leaving her alone in the kitchen with Ian.

"Would ye like some coffee?" she offered.

"Yes, but I can get it," he said, rising. "Those cookies sure smell good."

Isobeille laughed as she lifted a few carefully off the pan and onto the cooling rack. "Menfolk," she said, shaking her head. "Ye are all lads at heart when it comes te sweets, aye?"

"I suppose we are," Ian said, smiling. "Does that mean you'll share?"

"Och, I suppose her ladies' group willnae miss a few." Isobeille placed a couple of the still-warm cookies on a small plate and placed it in front of him.

"Ian Douglas Anderson," Mrs. Anderson mock-scolded when she returned to the kitchen. "Have you been eating cookies before dinner?"

Ian did his best to look innocent, but the dab of chocolate at the corner of his mouth gave him away. Isobeille tried not to laugh, but failed miserably, earning her a narrow-eyed look from the braw Scot.

"I didn't want to," Ian said, unable to completely hide his smile, "but she put the plate right in front of me. I thought it would have been rude to refuse. You taught me better than that, Mother."

Mrs. Anderson gave in to the urge to laugh, her blue eyes twinkling. "I guess I did at that."

"Ye both look verra bonnie in yer finery," Isobeille complimented, sliding the last of the cookies into a decorative tin and removing the thick oven mitts. Despite their obvious difference in height, it was clear to see that they were mother and son in their coloring and shared features.

"Thank you, dear," Mrs. Anderson said. As Isobeille wiped up the counter, she suddenly asked, "Isobeille, dear, why don't you join us for dinner?"

Ian piped in right away, "A wonderful idea, Mom. It will give us a chance to get to know each other a little better. What do you say, Isobeille?"

"Oh, I couldnae," Isobeille protested.

"Why not?" Mrs. Anderson asked bluntly.

"You said Nick has other plans for the night -" she frowned a bit at this "- and there's really no point to sitting around all by yourself when you could be having a nice dinner with us."

"I couldnae impose."

"Nonsense," Mrs. Anderson waved. "No imposition at all, and we really would love to have you."

Isobeille bit at her bottom lip; she was in a bit of a quandary, it seemed. It would be rude to ask to stay in Mrs. Anderson's apartment while she and her son went out, and she couldn't very well return to Nick's, not with the she-devil still over there (her initial impression of Nick's beloved had started low and plummeted steadily downward over the last hour or so). The thought of spending the next couple of hours lurking in the stairwell did not appeal to her at all.

Mayhap it would be fun to go out to one of these dining establishments. Mrs. Anderson was always pleasant to be around and her son seemed quite nice as well. If nothing else, it might serve as a distraction to keep her from imagining Nick in the arms of that woman. Hopefully, by the time the meal was over, Isobeille would be able to return safely to the apartment without fear of an unwanted encounter - assuming Nick didn't bring her back with him, that was. Since Isobeille found that too painful to contemplate, she pushed that particular thought aside.

She did have one worriment, however. Mrs. Anderson was wearing a pretty skirt with a silk blouse and matching jacket; Ian had on navy blue slacks and a dress shirt and tie. Even Isobeille knew enough to realize that her flour-dusted, casual garments were unacceptable for such an occasion.

"Thank ye, but I doona have the proper clothing."

"Our reservations aren't for an hour yet. Why don't you go next door and change?"

As if on cue, Isobeille heard the muffled sound of a door slamming – Nick's door – and knew that he must have just gotten home. Instead of her being there to greet him, someone else awaited him. Someone who Isobeille had absolutely no desire to see again anytime soon.

"Oh, ah, I cannae," she said quickly, feeling the warmth flood her face. "Nick's, uh, lady friend came to surprise him earlier, and I doona think they have quite left for the party yet…"

Ian politely looked away. Mrs. Anderson came as close to scowling as Isobeille had ever seen.

"That one," Mrs. Anderson said, shaking her head. "I don't know what he sees in her. Well, that clinches it, then. You're definitely coming with us. Come on, dear. I'm sure we can find something for you to wear."

* * *

By the time he opened the door to his apartment, he'd all but convinced himself to call Gloria and tell her he couldn't make it. The timing sucked, but maybe it was past due. Things just weren't working out, and -

"Well hello there, stranger," Gloria purred, greeting him in a matching red satin bra and panties. "I've missed you."

"Gloria!" Nick said, caught completely off-guard. "What are you doing here? Where's Isobeille? And why the hell are you dressed like that?"

Gloria pouted slightly, temporarily suspending the kisses she was planting along his jaw. "I think that would be obvious - I'm seducing you. And if you're talking about that little cleaning girl, I gave her the afternoon off. Sent her home early so we could be alone."

Cleaning girl? Home? This was Isobeille's home, he thought frantically. Then he remembered that Isobeille would probably just go next door to Mrs. Anderson's. Clearly she hadn't told Gloria who she was or that she was staying here with him, and he was thankful for that. This was his mess, and he should be the one to clean it up.

"Gloria, we need to talk."

Chapter 13

"You look beautiful," Ian said approvingly when Isobeille reappeared with his mother a short while later. Dressed in an ankle-length green skirt and white cashmere sweater, she looked stunning. Mrs. Anderson had gathered Isobeille's hair up into clips in an artful design, allowing a few curled tendrils to cascade down and frame her face.

"Thank ye," Isobeille blushed. "Ye are verra kind."

"I will be the envy of every man in the restaurant, having not one, but two such beauties on my arm this evening."

Isobeille's blush deepened, and Mrs. Anderson tittered. "He always was such a charmer," she told Isobeille. "Just like his father."

Ian opened the door, then motioned for the women to precede him. In an old-fashioned gesture, he held out his arm for Isobeille while his mother ensured the apartment was securely locked. Together, the trio headed toward the elevator.

As they waited for the car to arrive, Isobeille tried to think of a viable excuse for taking the stairs. Thus far she had avoided the infernal contraption;

Nick had been very accommodating about that, even though she knew he would have preferred the ride to the seven-flight descent and climb.

The sound of Nick shouting out Gloria's name just inside his apartment door was enough to temporarily halt the polite conversation taking place as Mrs. Anderson, Ian, and Isobeille waited for the elevator. The moment the doors slid open, Isobeille forgot all about her dislike of tight, enclosed spaces, and practically dove inside. She kept her head down, unwilling to see the looks on either of her companions' faces, or for them to see hers.

* * *

Nick struggled to think clearly, but that was all but impossible to do when he had a nearly naked woman intent on relieving him of his clothes against the back of his front door. Grabbing his shirt at the neckline, she wrenched the sides apart, sending buttons scattering across the floor.

"Gloria! What the hell has gotten into you?" he said. He stepped back, but since he was only just inside the doorway, that put him right up against the door.

"I missed you, Nick," she said, her long red nails raking across his shoulders, down his chest.

"Maybe we should - "

"Oh, yes, we definitely should," Gloria purred, leaning over to suck one of his now-exposed nipples into her mouth.

"Fuck!" he cursed. He grabbed her by the shoulders to push her away, but her hands were already making short work on unfastening his jeans. Before he knew what was happening, his pants and his briefs were down around his ankles.

"GLORIA!" he bellowed, pushing her backward.

"What?" she said, stubbornly reaching for him with her talon-like, manicured hands. "It's been a long time, Nick. Let me - "

"No," he said firmly. He released his shoulders and bent down to pull up his pants. Was he in the freaking Twilight Zone or something? Not once in the six months they'd been exclusive had she ever been lying in wait for him like that. She was by no means shy when it came to sex, but this was, well, over the top, even for her.

"You know," she said angrily, "most men would love to come home to a greeting like that."

Nick wasn't most men. And while he might have had a recent fantasy or two about just such a thing, it hadn't been Gloria he'd pictured doing the greeting.

"Jesus, Gloria. You just... you caught me off guard."

She continued to stare at him, but some of the anger faded, replaced with confusion. "What's with you, Nick? A month ago you would have bent me over the couch by now."

It was true; he couldn't deny it. But a month ago, he'd been thinking that he and Gloria had a future. Before she'd told him she wasn't ready. Before Isobeille had come into his life and changed the way he thought and felt about *everything*.

"Look, Gloria, I'm sorry," he started. It wasn't exactly the way he had planned on telling her, but maybe it was for the best. "I didn't mean - "

"No," she said, before he could finish the thought, "*I'm* sorry. I hurt you, Nick. You asked me to go to your parents with you, and I ... panicked."

Nick didn't know which stunned him more – the fact that Gloria had attacked him in his doorway or the fact that she was apologizing for blowing him off.

"I know I haven't made things easy for you, Nick, but I... I've had a lot of time to think about things and... I think I'm ready now."

Holy shit. Now she decides she's ready? After she spent the last couple of weeks cutting him off, making him feel like a loser for wanting something more?

"We should probably have a talk about that, Gloria. About us."

For the first time, he saw uncertainty in her eyes but she covered it up quickly. She nodded. "Yes," she agreed, "we probably should. But not now. You need a shower, and we'll already be fashionably late as it is."

"You still want to go?" he asked doubtfully.

"I have to, Nick. It's not really an option."

Maybe she had to, but he didn't. As if reading his mind, she said quietly, "You promised, Nick. And you look so handsome in your tux…"

* * *

"So tell me a little about yourself, Isobeille," Ian said, pronouncing her name with perfect inflection, lifting the carafe to pour another glass of wine for his mother first, then Isobeille. Unused to hearing it spoken correctly, Isobeille turned surprised eyes upon him, only to find his eyes twinkling.

"My son specializes in medieval Celtic and Norse cultures," Mrs. Anderson beamed.

"Do ye now?" Isobeille eagerly joined the conversation in an attempt to silence Nick's echoed shout in her mind. Up until that moment, she had continued to harbor the hope that Nick might change his mind about going to the party, about going out with Gloria. That wishful thinking had been accompanied by a particularly gratifying visualization of Nick showing the tall, slim-hipped blonde the door.

"Yes," Ian confirmed. "I did my thesis on the sociological, economic, and political ramifications of the death of King David I after his twelfth century reign."

"King David was a good mon, but I am partial te Robert II," Isobeille replied, taking a sip of her wine. It was quite delicious, she thought, and liked how it warmed her up on the inside and slightly dulled the surprisingly sharp ache that seemed to have taken up residence near the base of her rib cage and made it difficult to breathe. "King David was a wee bit before my time, I am afraid."

Ian's eyes opened wide and Mrs. Anderson clapped her hands together. "I just knew you two would hit it off!"

"Beauty and brains," Ian said with a smile. "I'm impressed. Please, Isobeille, tell me more."

Isobeille smiled shyly and sipped her wine, but inside, her heart was breaking.

* * *

Nick fastened his cuff links and looked at himself in the mirror. He looked like a man on his way to the gallows. Felt like one, too. Perhaps he was being overly dramatic. An evening of wining, dining, and dancing at a five-star hotel wasn't quite the same, but at that moment, it was close enough.

What was Isobeille doing now, he wondered? Was she still making cookies? Or had she and Mrs. Anderson finished, and were simply relaxing and chatting and enjoying one another's company?

What he wouldn't give to be doing just that right now. He missed her. It seemed kind of silly, really. He had seen her only that morning. They had had breakfast together, and she had proudly handed him his lunch and kissed him on the cheek, wishing him a good and safe day.

The thought made him smile. He wondered if she had any idea how much better his days were recently, because of things like that.

There was a quick knock on his bedroom door. "Nick, come on. We've got to go," Gloria said impatiently.

He exhaled heavily. Enough stalling. He could do this. Just a couple of hours. Then he could come back here and forget it ever happened. As he shut off the lights and picked up his wallet, the irony of the situation finally hit him. For months he had done everything right, had gone out of his way to treat Gloria like the special woman he'd thought she was, and Gloria hadn't appreciated any of it. Now that he wasn't returning her calls or welcoming her advances, she was interested.

All that time he'd been trying to figure out a way to win Gloria's heart, and it turned out all he'd had to do was treat her like shit.

Well, hell.

* * *

"I've never been on a horse-drawn carriage ride before," Ian admitted. "It's something I've wanted to do each time I visit, but this is my first time."

"'Tis lovely," Isobeille agreed beside him. "Why did ye not do it before?"

"I never had anyone willing to go with me," he said with a slightly crooked grin that was really quite charming. "Mother's terrified of horses," he confided with a wink. "Thank you, by the way, for indulging her suggestion that you join me. My mother is a lot of things, but no one has ever accused her of being subtle."

Isobeille laughed softly. Yes, she had been aware of what Mrs. Anderson had been doing, but she didn't mind. It was a nice diversion, and Ian was pleasant company.

Isobeille was not quite ready to return to Nick's apartment just yet. All had appeared to be quiet when they'd returned from dinner, but that didn't mean they weren't there, and Isobeille had no desire to walk in on anything. Overhearing just the little bit she had in the hallway had been more than enough; she did not think her heart would withstand actually seeing them together.

The carriage made its way around the outer edge of the park, where many of the trees were adorned with festive lights. A light snow had begun, creating prismatic halos around the streetlamps in the darkness. Isobeille tried to appreciate it; it was really a beautiful sight, making everything look clean and fresh and new, but it was hard to do so when it felt like there was a huge block of ice in her belly, painful and numbing at the same time.

"Are you warm enough?" Ian asked, tucking the small blanket around her legs.

"Oh, aye. Thank ye."

"I had a wonderful evening," Ian said. "You're the first woman I have ever met capable of discussing my thesis with me. Most would have fallen asleep after I told them the title of it."

Isobeille laughed softly, if a little sadly. "'Tis a topic near te my heart."

"What region of Scotland did you say you were from?"

"Gwynnevael."

Ian's eyes widened slightly, but Isobeille was too busy watching the snowflakes to notice. "I'm not familiar with that one. Is that near Inverness? or Edinburgh?"

"'Tis a small village in the Highlands, not close te anything, really, but I suppose 'tis nearer te Inverness. I remember visiting the loch there once; 'twas not so far of a journey, a few days at most." Her expression grew wistful. "Lots of rolling hills and craggy rocks. Forests I used te play in as a wee lass. More stars in the night sky than I could count in a hundred lifetimes."

"It sounds beautiful. Do you miss it?"

"Sometimes," she smiled sadly. "'Twas a far quieter life. Simpler. Here, there are so many people. So much noise and light and the smells, och! I find myself longing for the scent of pine and heather and cows. Sometimes I doona ken how ye can stand it, all this."

Ian nodded thoughtfully. "I know exactly what you mean. That's why I've got a little place up the coast. It's not much really, but it's remote, peaceful. It's too far to commute to the University every day, but I try to get up there on the weekends at least. I love listening to the ocean, especially at night."

"Ye paint quite a lovely picture. I have never seen the ocean."

Ian wondered briefly how a woman could travel from Scotland to America via conventional means and *not* see the ocean, but thought it might be rude to ask. He was having such a nice time with Isobeille; he didn't want to do anything to ruin it.

"Not to sound too forward or anything, but I'd be happy to take you there sometime. It's rather cold this time of year, but at least you would get to see the ocean. If you'd like."

"Aye," Isobeille said in that gentle way of hers. "I think I would at that. Thank ye."

"What about your friend?" Ian prodded. "Will he mind?"

Isobeille's features softened for a moment, but she quickly veiled any expression that might have come after. "Nick? Nay, I doona think so. He has his own life, ye ken. He is too kind te say so, but sometimes I feel naught but a burden."

Ian didn't openly contradict her; after all, he knew next to nothing about his mother's next door neighbor and even less about his relationship with Isobeille, but after spending just a few hours in her company, he couldn't conceive of Isobeille being a burden to anyone. She was intelligent, kind, soft-spoken, and well-mannered. She had a quick wit and just a hint of subtle mischief about her that made her interesting and pleasant to be around.

Yet for all that, he sensed a terrible sadness in her, one that she went to great efforts to conceal. His mother had told him that she was all alone, that except for Nick and her, Isobeille knew no one. Ian understood that, being rather a solitary guy himself, but at least he had some friends and family he could turn to when he got to feeling a bit lonely.

"Do you still have family there? In Gwynnevael, I mean?"

Sorrow shadowed her delicate features once again. After six hundred years, it was unlikely that any of her bloodline remained. As far as she knew, she was all that remained of the McKenna clan.

"When I left my home, my father was still alive," she said carefully, "but he has since passed."

"I'm sorry."

"Thank ye. We dinnae get on verra weel, but he was the only kinsmon I had."

"I understand," Ian said softly. "My mother is all I have left."

Isobeille looked up then, right into his eyes.

"Ye are a bonnie mon, and a successful one as weel," she said with all sincerity. "Surely ye will marry and have a family."

Ian laughed. "Well, thank you, but I wasn't kidding when I said you were the first woman able to sit through a full meal with me without looking catatonic by the end. I'm not very good company, I'm afraid."

"Ye are fine company," Isobeille said firmly, patting his hand reassuringly. "And quite charming, as weel. There are many a fine lass who would be tickled te be sharing this carriage with ye. If ye want to talk *boring*, ye should sit through three days of reckoning at Michaelmas."

He laughed again. "Not all women are as easy to talk to as you are, Isobeille. You really are a rare delight."

"I like the way ye speak my name," she said quietly. "It reminds me of my home. Would ye mind saying it again?"

"*Isobeille.*"

"Thank ye for that."

"My pleasure."

Chapter 14

It was well after one a.m. when Gloria finally decided enough of the right people had left so that she could, too. She tracked Nick down, finding him at the bar on his cell phone. Again. Several times over the course of the evening, he'd retreated into an alcove and pulled out the small device.

"Who are you calling?" she asked point-blank.

Nick scowled and returned the phone to his pocket. "Just checking messages," he said evasively.

He'd called Mrs. Anderson's to check on Isobeille shortly after they'd arrived at the party, leaving a message when no one answered. Then he'd called again later, and a coolly polite Mrs. Anderson told him not to worry, that Isobeille was just fine. When Nick asked to speak with her, his neighbor told him that she couldn't come to the phone, but wouldn't say why. Frustrated, he'd asked Mrs. Anderson to have Isobeille call him, but so far, she hadn't. Now it was too late to call again, but he was sorely tempted.

If he could just talk to Isobeille, hear her voice

and know that she was alright, he'd feel so much better. She was like a drug, he realized, and he'd missed his evening Isobeille-fix. He had been looking forward to spending a little bit of time with her before having to leave for this damn party, maybe sharing a quick supper, but Gloria had been lying in wait for him, shooting that plan all to hell.

And that was yet another reason why he was anxious to talk to Isobeille. What exactly had Gloria said to her? How had Isobeille reacted? Was she angry with him? Is that why she wasn't returning his calls? And where the hell was she that she couldn't talk to him earlier? Had Mrs. Anderson even given her the message or told her that he'd called?

"Nick? Did you hear me?"

Nick glanced up to find Gloria beside him, looking annoyed.

"Sorry. What?"

Gloria rolled her eyes. "I'm ready to leave."

"About time," he mumbled. He'd had more than enough of this; all he wanted to do was go home and see Isobeille.

He walked toward the exit, Gloria trailing a step or two behind. A few weeks ago, Nick would have waited and walked to the door with Gloria at his side. Now Nick was too interested in getting the hell out of there to care.

Nick paused outside the doors and caught sight of a man about a block down, playing *Carol of the*

Bells on a beat-up looking acoustic guitar. Pulling a twenty out of his pocket, Nick walked straight toward him and dropped it into the bucket he had sitting next to him.

"Bless you," the man said with a nod.

"Come *on*, Nick," Gloria said, pulling at his sleeve while shooting the musician a look of pure disdain. "It's cold out here."

"Yeah, it is. Imagine how he feels." Thinking of the night he and Isobeille helped that man in the alley, Nick took off his scarf and gave it to the man as well.

Gloria sniffed. "His choice, not mine."

Nick stiffened. "I don't think he *chose* to get laid off, Gloria. And the only reason he *chooses* to be out here at one o'clock in the morning is probably so he can make a couple of bucks to feed his kids."

"Yeah, right. Hit the bar, more like. God, Nick. When are you going to stop letting people walk all over you?"

An excellent question, that, Nick thought. He glanced over his shoulder at the guitar player, who was now looking at *him* with sympathy.

"Did that girl give you some bullshit sob story, too? Is that why you gave her a job? I hope you've got everything locked up when you go to work. She's probably robbing you blind."

Nick barked out a laugh. Isobeille, steal? The very idea was ludicrous. The woman was the most giving, caring soul he'd ever met.

"My place or yours?" Gloria asked, wrapping her hands around his neck as they waited for the doorman to call them a cab. As if she hadn't just spent the last block reaming his ass for being a sucker.

"Neither," said Nick, removing her hands. "I can't."

He'd had more than he could take. All he wanted to do was go home, wash away the stench of Gloria's cloying perfume, and spend the rest of the night trying to make it up to Isobeille. Guilt weighed heavily on his shoulders; he never should have agreed to this, commitment or not. He and Gloria, it just wasn't working. It wasn't right. Not like it was with Isobeille.

"Can't or won't?" Gloria snapped, then seemed to think better of it as a cab arrived and Nick held the door open for her. Once they were inside, her voice softened and she slid next to him on the seat.

"You're not still mad, are you, Nicky? 'Cause I can adjust your attitude..." To accentuate her point, she placed her hand on his inner thigh and slid it upwards to cup him. Gently, but firmly, he removed it.

"I'm not mad, Gloria. I'm just... done."

"That's okay. We don't have to do anything more tonight." She nipped at his ear and grinned wickedly. "If I remember correctly, you're more of a morning person anyway."

"No, Gloria." *Not again. Ever.*

Gloria's grin was instantly replaced with a scowl. She pulled back, but kept her hands possessively on his arm.

"What's with you, Nick? Last month you wanted to take me home to meet your mother. Now you don't even want to spend the night. What gives?"

Nick exhaled heavily. He'd been asking himself the same question all day. He wished he had an answer that made sense, but the one explanation he kept coming back to scared the shit out of him. So he went with what he hoped sounded logical.

"Look, Gloria. You made it very clear that you didn't want to rush into anything. And you were right. Now I'm just asking for some of the same."

Gloria narrowed her eyes. "This is about that little redhead I found in your kitchen today, isn't it? She's doing more than your cooking and cleaning, isn't she? Are you sleeping with her, Nick?"

Nick's features hardened. "No. And leave her out of it. She has nothing to do with this."

It was a huge lie. Isobeille had everything to do with this. Because of Isobeille, he was finally seeing things clearly. Because of her, he finally knew what he wanted.

What was really important.

And it wasn't Gloria, or getting into med school, or fancy parties with hors d'oevres and designer clothes. It was hot chocolate and taking long walks and caring enough for someone to put their needs and wants above your own.

"She's the one from the video, isn't she, Nick? The one you pushed out of the way of that bus! I knew that little bitch looked familiar! Jesus, Nick! What are you going to tell me next, that she's living with you?"

Nick clenched his teeth together so tightly he was afraid a few molars might snap. "Shut up, Gloria. You have no idea what you're talking about."

"This *is* all about her, isn't it?" she pressed.

"No, it isn't. *This* is about you only having time for me when it's convenient for you. *This* is about you getting everything you want without giving anything in return."

"I don't know how you can say that."

"You don't? Then let me enlighten you, because I've been giving this a lot of thought lately…"

* * *

Ian remained quietly just inside the door while Isobeille gathered a few things. She'd had every intention of returning to Nick's apartment, but changed her mind when she had seen the state of things: buttons all over the floor, flowers laying crushed and wilted among them; the lamp on the table just inside the door, knocked askew, a square condom packet in plain view next to it.

Mrs. Anderson, of course, was more than glad to have Isobeille spend the night, and Ian felt better about it, too.

"Ian?" Isobeille stopped him at the door before he left.

"Yes?"

"Thank ye."

"For what?"

She gave him a sad smile. She knew that their after-dinner activities had had nothing whatsoever to do with Ian getting his first carriage ride and everything with providing a distraction, to keep her from thinking about Nick and what had transpired.

"I want ye to have this. 'Tis not much, I ken, but 'tis all I have te give ye."

"Isobeille, you don't have to give me anything," he protested, but he felt her press something cool and heavy into his hand. He opened his palm and looked at the coin, his eyes widening.

"Since ye are a professor and all, this might have some meaning for ye."

It took a moment for Ian to find his voice. He knew what he held in his hand. "Isobeille, this is… priceless."

Isobeille closed his fingers around it with her own. "I want ye to have it. Please."

"I don't know what to say."

"Say ye will take me te see the ocean

tomorrow, Ian."

"It would be my great pleasure, Isobeille," he said with a smile. Then he saw her safely into his mother's apartment and wished her a good night.

*** * ***

By the time Nick got back to his place, he felt drained, but better. Lighter. He'd broken things off with Gloria; he hadn't realized how much that had been weighing on him. It had been a hellish day, and he was more than ready for it to end. It was time to move on, and he was going to start with a hot shower and hopefully finish on the couch with Isobeille – assuming she wasn't too angry with him, that was.

The apartment was dark and quiet. He knew the moment he walked in that Isobeille wasn't there. The place felt emptier than it ever had. He'd become so used to her presence, so accustomed to walking through the door to find her waiting for him with a smile, it felt strange to be in his own apartment without her.

He flipped on the light, no longer worried about waking Isobeille. What he saw made him wince. The flowers he'd bought for Isobeille lay wilted and crushed just inside the door, along with his belt and the scattered buttons from his shirt. The roast she had lovingly prepared for him sat burned and dried atop the stove, forgotten.

He hoped upon hope that Isobeille had not come back to the apartment tonight; that she had just elected to stay with Mrs. Anderson, because he didn't want to think about her seeing any of this. Even though he knew nothing had actually happened, it sure looked like it had. As he righted the lamp, he spotted the unopened condom – no doubt placed there by Gloria in preparation for her surprised seduction - and groaned.

Postponing his shower, he went about cleaning up the mess first instead.

He threw open the windows, letting the icy air clear away Gloria's lingering, heavy perfume. He swept up the wilted flowers and buttons, emptying the dust pan into the trash. Then he tipped the remains of what would have been his dinner into the trash and did the dishes. When that was all done he tied up the trash bag and carried it down to the bin, not wanting any reminder of the evening in his apartment when Isobeille returned in the morning. If she even wanted to.

Well, he told himself, if she didn't, he was going to do his damnedest to convince her otherwise.

He looked at the tiny Christmas tree sitting in the corner and sighed. It was what his mom would have called a "Charlie Brown tree". Isobeille stared at that thing for hours; she'd asked him to place it where she could see it as she fell asleep at night and be the first thing she saw in the morning.

It seemed wrong to have it sitting in the dark like that, so Nick plugged in the strands of lights. So simply decorated, with its tiny little lights and hand-crafted bows, lovingly made by a woman who knew the true spirit of Christmas and held it in her heart every day of the year.

And yet, despite its size and its simplicity, it was quite possibly the most beautiful tree he had ever seen.

Only then did he take a shower and crawl onto the sofa, pulling the pillow and blanket up to his nose. They smelled like Isobeille – like snow and wildflowers.

Sleep was a long time in coming. The events of the day kept rolling around in his head. There were so many things he should have done differently, but there was little he could do about that now. All he could do was try to make everything right again.

Eventually he fell into a tormented sleep around dawn.

Chapter 15

"May I come in?" Nick asked.

Mrs. Anderson opened the door, allowing him to step into her apartment. "Isobeille isn't here," she said, her face devoid of the welcoming, neighborly smile she usually had for him.

"She isn't?" Nick asked, fear settling in to the pit of his stomach. "She didn't spend the night here with you?"

"Yes, she did, but she's gone now."

"Gone? Gone where?"

Mrs. Anderson fixed him with a stern look. "Away for the day. It will do her good."

Away? Where the hell would Isobeille go? The thought of her out there in the city all alone filled his veins with icy dread.

"Mrs. Anderson, this is really important. Please tell me where she is."

"Let me ask you something first," Mrs. Anderson said. "Why is it so important to you? Isobeille is a grown woman, and you, obviously, are involved with someone else."

"Not anymore," Nick said, his jaw flexing. The way Mrs. Anderson was looking at him like a pissed-off mother hen, she *knew*. Which meant that Isobeille probably did, too.

Nick was a big boy; he knew he'd messed up and would face the consequences. But he would have done anything if he could have somehow prevented hurting Isobeille's feelings. The thought of seeing that wounded look in her eyes was cutting him up on the inside. He would never forgive himself if something happened to her because he had been too dense to see what had been right before his eyes.

"Isobeille may be a grown woman, but in many ways she is like a child. She's been... sheltered."

Nick struggled to find a way to explain to the older woman that Isobeille was not a typical twenty-four year old woman without revealing the whole truth or sounding like a nut case.

"She isn't familiar with city life. There are those that will take advantage of her."

Mrs. Anderson pinned him with a gimlet eye. He'd seen that same look on his own mother's face every time he or one of his siblings had done something incredibly stupid. Nick should have foreseen that Isobeille would bring out those primitive, protective instincts in her. Hadn't he been feeling those same instincts since day one?

"Like men who might expect her to clean and cook for them, and hide away in an apartment all day by herself until they come home from work?" she asked. "Except, of course, when those men plan on inviting their lady friends over – and I use the term lady quite loosely here – and expect her to conveniently disappear for several hours?"

Nick winced. "It's not like that."

Mrs. Anderson raised an eyebrow and crossed her arms over her chest. "Is that so? How is it, then?"

"Isobeille needed a place to stay. She was new in town, didn't know anyone, had no place to go. I was trying to help." He ran his hand through his hair. "I never asked her to clean or cook or do any of those things – she wanted to, said it made her feel useful."

But he had loved it, hadn't he? Knowing he'd come home to a warm, clean apartment and a home-cooked meal. But mostly, he realized now, it was knowing that Isobeille was waiting for him that he loved the most.

Mrs. Anderson's features softened a little. "Maybe you were trying to help. Most people would have just turned their backs on her, or dropped her off at a shelter and let someone else worry about her. But did you ever stop to think that she might mistake what you saw as simple kindness and human compassion for something… more?"

God, his chest hurt. "She knew I had a girlfriend. I never lied about that. And despite what you might think, I never, uh, seduced her." He clamped his mouth shut, mortified. What on earth had ever possessed him to share that with his neighbor?

Mrs. Anderson shook her head sadly. "You don't understand anything, do you? You think because you didn't try to blatantly get her into your bed – and I am quite proud of you for that, by the way – that you were not seducing her? A woman like Isobeille would have seen through something like that in a heartbeat."

"What are you saying? That I seduced a woman *un*intentionally?"

"Oh, I don't think it was truly unintentional. I think some part of you recognized what Isobeille was to you even while your head was up your – well, let's just say your head was in a much darker place."

Her mouth quirked up at the corners. She seemed much happier now that Nick was miserable and squirming.

Nick looked the older woman directly in the eyes and held her gaze. "And what do you think Isobeille is to me?" he asked softly.

She didn't hesitate. "Why, your one true love, of course."

The ache in his chest increased; drawing a full breath became difficult. He wondered vaguely if it was the beginning of a heart attack, then dismissed the idea. He was still having trouble wrapping his head around Mrs. Anderson's words.

"I don't believe in that stuff."

"Just because you choose not to believe doesn't

mean it isn't real. Isobeille knows it, too." Mrs. Anderson's eyes glistened. "Why else do you think she would have travelled through time to find you?"

* * *

Isobeille's opinion of automobiles changed drastically as they made their way up the coast. She liked Ian's convertible Audi GT Spyder very much; it was nothing at all like the cramped and malodorous taxi.

"Are you sure you're not too cold?" he asked.

"Nay! 'Tis invigorating! Like riding upon a fine stallion at full gallop, but without the pain in the backside!"

Ian laughed. It felt good to smile again, even if she was hurting inside.

It took slightly more than two hours to reach Ian's place along the cape, but the ride passed quickly. Isobeille loved the stereo, amazed at the choices of music genres available. She spent a lot of time playing with all the buttons – much to Ian's amusement – stopping when she found a song she liked. She seemed as equally fond of rock ballads as she was techno-pop and classical – some of which had her dancing in her seat.

"Ye live here alone?" Isobeille asked uncertainly, eyeing the size of the house. It looked much larger than she had imagined. Ian had made it sound quite modest, but it didn't appear that way to her, a woman who had grown up in a small, two-room dwelling.

"Yes, just me," he said, carrying her small bag and his into the foyer. "Would you like a tour?"

"Aye!" she said excitedly.

Ian's bungalow had none of the plain white walls and clean lines that Nick's apartment had. Dark, rich colors and wood paneling covered the walls – those that weren't already covered in bookshelves, that is. The furniture, too, was plush and dark; the woodwork was intricately carved and polished. The slight lingering scent of wood smoke mingled with that of lemon oil and old books.

"'Tis the most beautiful house I have ever seen," Isobeille breathed as each room seemed even better than the last. She ran her hands lovingly along the leather-bound volumes strewn everywhere. It was warm and cozy and very lived in. Ian's presence was evident in every room – masculine, scholarly, and tasteful.

"Ye must be verra wealthy te have such a fine place like this."

"I do alright," he said modestly. "Come. There's something I'd like you to see."

Isobeille followed Ian through an attractive kitchen of dark wood and stainless steel and out onto a large deck that ran the entire width of the bungalow and wrapped around each corner. Isobeille walked out to the railing and looked out onto the ocean.

"'Tis so verra big," she murmured, her eyes wide with wonder at the sight before her.

Ian laughed. "Yes, it is. Would you like to go down to the water?"

"Oh, aye! Please!"

Ian took her hand and led her down the steps toward the rocks that formed the shore along his property. Much to his dismay, Isobeille wasted no time in removing her shoes and socks and wading out into the ocean, despite the fact that the water was ice cold. She seemed so genuinely excited, he didn't have the heart to stop her. He did, however, ensure that her little foray into the freezing waters was not a long one.

Even later, when she was still shivering and Ian had tucked a blanket around her legs and placed a steaming mug of hot chocolate into her hands, Isobeille was still smiling.

"What do ye call these little white things?" she asked. Ian was forced to hide his smile at the prominent white mustache adorning her upper lip.

"Marshmallows," he said. Deliberately, he tilted his own mug so that he was sporting a similar 'stache. Isobeille's eyes widened, then giggled as she reached up to confirm that she, too, had one.

"Marshmallows," she repeated. "I like marshmallows verra much."

"I thought you might." The cocoa and the shots of Bailey's he'd added should have her warmed up in no time.

"Thank ye, Ian, for bringing me te yer home and showing me the ocean. Ye are a verra kind mon."

"You are very welcome, Isobeille. But I'm not quite as selfless as you might think. I had an ulterior motive for bringing you here today."

For the first time since she had met him, Isobeille felt a twinge of unease, but it was gone as quickly as it had come. Yes, she was alone in a house with a man she had only met the night before, but Ian was not a man with evil in his heart. She'd been around enough of those to know the difference, at least.

"Aye? And what might that be?"

"I was hoping," Ian said carefully, "that you might share with me what life was truly like in early fifteenth-century Scotland."

She smiled serenely, but he did not miss the flash in her eyes. "Ye are the expert, Ian. I am no scholar."

"No," he agreed. "You are something much better. You are someone who's actually *lived* it."

Chapter 16

Nick stared at Mrs. Anderson, his face frozen into a mask of neutrality. He wasn't sure if he should laugh out loud or sigh in relief. She made the decision for him.

"It's alright, Nick. I'm not crazy. Well, not about this, anyway. I know Isobeille is not from our time."

Despite her assurances, Nick was reluctant to admit anything just yet. "Did she tell you that?"

"No. I suspect you are the only one she has trusted enough with that information."

"Then how…"

"Do I know?" Mrs. Anderson finished for him. "Well, let's just say I've been around long enough to know that anything is possible. Oh, I had my suspicions, of course. I knew from the first time I met the girl that she was, well, *different*. But it didn't all become clear to me until last night."

"My son, Ian, has several degrees, including two doctorates in medieval Scottish and Norse history," she explained. "He is considered by many to be one of the world's foremost experts on the subject, as a matter of fact. It is one of the reasons I asked him to come down to see me. I wanted him to meet Isobeille."

Something uncomfortable twisted in Nick's gut. "And did he?"

The older woman's eyes glittered. "Oh, yes. He was quite taken with her."

That uncomfortable twisting worsened, forming large, wiggling knots, but Mrs. Anderson continued happily, "They hit it off instantly, as I suspected they would. We went to dinner and had a lovely time. Then Ian coaxed her into a carriage ride around the park. That, apparently, went quite well, from what I gathered."

She pinned Nick with a glare that spoke volumes, but the short version of it was that she thought Nick was an idiot, and that her son would be a much better match for Isobeille.

"Did it?" he asked, his voice strained.

"Yes," she sighed. "It's a shame she's already head over heels in love with you. I would have liked to have had her as a daughter-in-law. As it is, she and Ian will just be great friends, I suppose."

Nick felt a flood of relief wash through him, but until he saw with his own two eyes that Isobeille was safe, until he could hold her in his arms again, he would not be content.

"Anyway, as I was saying," Mrs. Anderson looked pointedly at Nick as if he was the one who had gotten her off track, "Ian was all too willing to humor me. I don't think he believed me at first, but something happened in the past week that got him thinking. Someone from the University gave him an ancient coin and asked him to confirm its authenticity. Apparently it was in quite good condition, as if it had only been fashioned a few months ago instead of several centuries. After we spoke, he agreed to meet with Isobeille, to bring up various topics and see how she reacted, as well as pose several questions. A series of tests, I suppose, administered subtly and without her knowledge. Not surprisingly, he came to the same conclusion that I did."

Mrs. Anderson paused, her expression as determined and challenging as Nick had ever seen. "The question now, young man, is what are we going to do about it?"

* * *

"Do you have any idea how incredible this is for someone like me, who has spent the majority of the last ten years studying something I could only dream about?" Ian asked, his eyes dancing with excitement. "And here you are, a living, breathing example of what I've simply read about my whole life?"

Isobeille sipped her cocoa, averting her eyes. "Why do ye believe such a thing as fantastic as that?"

Ian smiled. "Remember when we were talking

at dinner last night? Nobody – and I mean nobody - could have known the things you knew without years of intensive study, and you already mentioned you'd never been to college. Several times I lapsed into an ancient dialect that hasn't been spoken for centuries, yet you didn't even blink. Plus you told me about your village – Gwynnevael? Gwynnevael ceased to exist half a millennium ago, yet I'd heard of that place once before. I couldn't remember where until my mother reminded me of an obscure reference in the ancestral history I started when I was still an undergrad. It was a passage from memoirs written by one of my ancestors – a knight by the name of Sir Galen Anderson. He wrote about the woman he was supposed to have married, but who mysteriously disappeared just before he could come for her."

Isobeille felt the blood draining from her face, but Ian was too excited to notice.

"He described her as having a gentle soul and the beauty of an angel, with hair the color of a fine garnet and eyes like cut emeralds. He called her his treasure, a treasure he'd unearthed in a tiny little village known as Gwynnevael."

"And yer ancestor," she said in a shaky voice. "Did he name his betrothed?"

"Yes," Ian said, his eyes sparkling. "Her name was Isobeille. Isobeille Aislinn McKenna."

* * *

"First things first," Mrs. Anderson said. "Do you love Isobeille?"

"Yes." The answer just came out, without hesitation, without thought. Nick was tired of trying to fool himself. He loved Isobeille, loved her with his heart and his mind and his soul.

"Good," Mrs. Anderson nodded approvingly. "It's about time you figured that out. What about that other woman you were seeing?"

"Gloria. That's over," he said, still a bit shaken by the realization that he was in love with Isobeille. Last night he'd finally realized that it wasn't really Gloria that he'd so desperately wanted, but a woman who he could share his life with. Someone who would make him laugh, and ask about his day, and sit in the dark and watch movies and fall asleep with him. Someone like Isobeille.

"Good. I never liked that woman."

Nick raised an eyebrow, but Mrs. Anderson just smirked. "Now that all of that's been taken care of, I guess that just leaves one last thing."

"What's that?"

"Why, proposing to Isobeille, of course."

* * *

"Isobeille, are you alright?"

Ian finally noticed that Isobeille was looking a little pale. He swapped her hot chocolate for a small decanter of brandy and told her to drink.

"Aye. 'Tis just a wee bit of a shock."

Ian waited until she had taken a couple of sips and the color began to return to her face. "I'm sorry. I'm afraid I got so caught up in things that I neglected to think about how all of this would affect you. I can't even imagine what you must be feeling right now."

"Weel," she said with a little smile, "A wee bit shocked, aye, but also verra grateful."

"How so?"

"Of all those who I might have encountered, I am verra fortunate te have been found by such kind and caring folk as Nick and yerself." She smiled. "And I would be honored te share with ye all that ye wish. For a price, of course," she added mischievously.

"Name it."

"I wish for some more of that hot chocolate with the wee marshmallows."

"I can do you one better than that," Ian said, his eyes lit with excitement. "I could really use a personal assistant. One who knows the ins and outs of medieval Scottish life, of course. She'd have to be intelligent, curious, and hard-working, as well as be able to sit through meetings and dinners and occasional travel with me as a companion. Do you know anyone who might be interested?"

For several moments, Isobeille could not breathe. "Ye... ye wish te offer me employment?"

Ian smiled and nodded. "I can't think of

anyone more qualified. It would pay a decent wage, but it would involve a lot of time and research on your part. Of course, I'm willing to negotiate the details..."

A job! Ian was offering her a job! She would earn a wage, be able to make a life for herself. "I accept," she said quickly, cutting off whatever else he was going to say.

"But I haven't even told you the terms of employment yet, or offered a salary."

"Doesnae matter. I accept."

Ian laughed at her enthusiasm. "We must work on your negotiating skills, Isobeille, but rest assured, I will see that you are well-compensated."

* * *

Nick had to keep himself from running to the door when he heard the key turning in the lock. He inhaled deeply, then checked his breath for freshness, smoothed his shirt, and ran his fingers nervously through his hair. A quick tap of his pocket assured him that his gift was still there.

"Isobeille," he said, breathing out her name in a whoosh of air. She looked even more beautiful than he remembered.

"Nick," she said cautiously, peering around. "Are ye alone?"

A pang of guilt ran through him. "Yeah. Did you have a good time with Ian?" He tried not to choke on the words. Tried not to groan out loud when Isobeille's eyes lit up like the goddamn Christmas tree at the mention of the other man's name.

"Aye. He is a verra nice mon. He kens a lot aboot my time. And, Nick, he offered me a job! A real one, where I will earn my own wage! I will no longer be a burden te ye."

Nick's heart ached. "Isobeille, you could never be a burden. Not to me."

For a moment, her eyes softened, but she looked away. Nick hated that he had done that to her, made her believe for even one second that she was anything less than a precious gift.

"He says he will help me get something called a *veeza*, so I can apply for a room at the university."

"I don't want you to leave," Nick blurted out.

Isobeille forced a smile, but it was the saddest, most insincere smile he'd ever seen. "Thank ye for that," she said carefully. "But 'tis for the best. I am certain your woman would agree."

"Actually, I, uh, broke up with Gloria. I'm sorry about the way she treated you. You won't ever have to see her again."

"Oh," she said, clearly surprised. "Is that a good thing? For ye, I mean?"

"It's a very good thing," he said, summoning the courage to close the space between them. He stopped when he was still a good two feet away. "It's something I should have done a long time ago."

Big green eyes looked up at him, swirling with the emotion she was trying so hard to hide. But she couldn't hide from him, not anymore. His eyes were wide open now, his vision crystal clear.

"And why is that?"

"Because. I don't love Gloria."

Her eyes widened slightly. "Ye doona?" she asked carefully, her voice little more than a breathy rush of air as she sought to control her breathing.

"No. As it happens, I'm in love with someone else."

"Oh." The spark of hope faded quickly as Isobeille shifted her weight from one foot to the other. "Then I guess I am happy for ye."

"Are you?" He took another step closer, close enough that he could feel the heat from her body, so that her delicate scent of snow and wildflowers, now also mixed with salt and sea, filled his lungs. It was like coming home.

Isobeille didn't answer.

"Isobeille?" he pressed softly. "Are you happy for me?"

"Nay," she said quietly, refusing to look at him. "I amnac."

Nick smiled at the top of her head. His sweet, honest Isobeille. He loved her so much his heart threatened to simply break free of his chest and lay itself right at her feet.

"What if I told you that the woman I love is

you? Would that make a difference in how you feel?"

Isobeille blinked, the fat tears that had yet to fall clinging to her lashes as she tilted her head up to look into his face. "Ye love... me?"

"Aye, that I do, sweet Isobeille," Nick said, taking her hands in his. Looking at her now, feeling the way he always felt in her presence, he couldn't believe it had taken him so long to figure that out. He reached for the words he'd looked up and had been practicing all day.

"*Isobeille, Tha gaol agam ort,*" he said, hoping he hadn't butchered the Scottish-Gaelic version of "I love you" too badly. "And I've been a blind fool not to realize that sooner."

Nick bent down on one knee before her. "But the important thing is that I do now, and I know the only woman I want to spend the rest of my life with is you. Will you marry me, Isobeille, and make me the happiest man on earth, in this time or any other?"

Chapter 17

Isobeille might have been a bit naïve; she might have been clueless when it came to living in the twenty-first century, but she was no fool. She looked down at the man now on bended knee before her, gazing up at her with those wonderful brown eyes. Once filled with kindness, they were now filled with something else, too - *love*.

All of her worries, all of her doubts, dissipated as the truth sank in. Nick loved her. He wanted to wed her and make her his bride. In those moments, her world was reduced to only the man in front her; everything, everyone else ceased to exist.

She placed her hand on his head, lightly stroking his mussed chestnut hair. It was the first time she had allowed herself to openly do so; it was even softer, silkier than she had imagined.

"Ye are a bonnie, fine mon, Nick Peterson," she said quietly.

Nick closed his eyes and leaned into her hand. Then opened them right back up again when he realized she hadn't said yes. "Isobeille?"

"A bonnie, fine mon, indeed," she murmured. One of her hands slipped into his hair, letting it slide between her fingers until she cupped him at the base of his neck. The other rested lightly on his shoulder. She stepped forward until his face was only a hair's breadth away from her bosom. It was a bold move, one meant to tempt and entice. She had seen his gaze alight there more than once, had seen the desire and hunger in his eyes.

* * *

Nick's heart began to pound against the walls of his chest as his lungs filled with the scent of Isobeille; he could feel the heat of her lush little body on his face just as tangibly as those light, curling strokes of her fingers against the back of his neck – the ones currently sending white-hot shivers up and down his spine. She was barely touching him, and yet his entire body hardened with an almost visceral need.

And then he felt it, felt her small hands exerting just the tiniest bit of gentle pressure, coaxing him closer. He looked up and saw her cheeks flushed with color, her eyes half-shuttered, her mouth just slightly agape in a silent, subtle plea. It was, quite possibly, the sexiest thing he had ever seen.

Unable to help himself, Nick moved his head slightly, nuzzling her breast. She made a sound somewhere in the back of her throat, a sound he'd never heard before but that somehow reached right down between them, grabbed him by the balls, and *squeezed.*

"Isobeille," he breathed. He wanted her so much, to claim her, to make her his. Did she know what she was doing to him? Did she know that her light, innocent touches lit a fire in his blood that he could barely contain?

Had she been anyone else, he would have been buried deep inside her body by now. But she wasn't. She was his Isobeille, sweet and gentle and so damn innocent. Despite the desperate need welling up within, he wanted more than sex. So much more. He wanted to spend the rest of his life loving her, caring for her, making sure she never felt lost or lonely or unhappy ever again.

No, he wouldn't ravage her like he wanted to. He would find the strength to leash his lust and let her set the pace of whatever happened next. He was hers to command, to do with what she wanted, as long as she said yes.

Which she had not yet done.

That realization penetrated his lusty thoughts. Why hadn't she said yes? She was still here, her luscious breasts only inches away from his hungry mouth, her fingers making light little circles that felt absolutely amazing against the back of his neck, her nails digging into his shoulder through the fabric of his shirt. Did she doubt his sincerity?

Or – his groin tightened painfully at the thought – did she seek to ensure that she owned him mind, body, and soul before accepting his proposal?

Because he was totally okay with that.

Leashing his baser instincts was one thing, but he couldn't completely quell the need to touch her. His hands found purchase on the curve of her hips. Sweet, curvy hips that he longed to feel bare beneath his hands.

Apparently she needed it, too. With a tiny gasp she pushed forward and tugged on his hair, making his scalp tingle.

"Aye, Nick," she breathed, her brogue more pronounced, his name little more than a guttural utterance on her lips.

It was all the encouragement he needed. He turned his head to the left, placing a light kiss upon the inside of her breast, right through her sweater. Then he turned and did the same to the other side. He slipped his hands just under the hem and caressed the smooth, bare flesh of her belly with his thumbs.

"More, Nick," she pleaded, pressing herself against him.

Fuck, yes. Isobeille might be innocent, but she was responsive as hell. Even the slightest caress seemed to bring out a passion in her that he had only dreamed of up until this point.

Lifting her top a little more, he pressed his face against her skin, reveled in the softness, the fragrance. He kissed her lightly, tiny little close-lipped kisses that made him yearn for a taste. Then he allowed his tongue to peak out and swirl around her belly button before dipping inside.

"Nick!" she gasped, tugging at his hair, which seemed to have a direct correlation to the pleasure centers in his groin.

With each passing second, Nick was losing more of his self-control. He needed Isobeille, needed her with a passion that threatened to burn him from the inside out. She was his. She had travelled six hundred years. *For him*. He'd been an idiot not to fully recognize that before now, but now that he did, there was no way he was ever letting her go.

"Isobeille, sweetheart, I love you. But if you aren't ready for this, you need to tell me now while I can still stop myself."

It was a lie, the biggest one he'd told yet. He couldn't stop now, not without doing some serious damage to his internal organs.

And his sanity.

* * *

Isobeille heard the words through the haze of desire clouding her mind. Nick's honor was an admirable thing, but if he thought to stop now, she might just not survive it.

"Doona cease. Doona *ever* cease."

He growled something against her belly, a wholly masculine series of sounds that made the internal muscles directly beneath his mouth clench. She thought she might have caught the words "thank" and "God" in there among some others, but she could not be sure and did not really care. The only thing that mattered was that he was no longer prattling on about that stopping nonsense.

The next moment, her world tilted even farther on its axis as Nick swept her off of her feet and tucked her against him.

She was only vaguely aware of entering his bedroom, too intent on holding on, on relishing the distinct rippling of his shoulders, arms, and chest as he carried her. Then she felt the soft give of the mattress beneath her, countered by the heavenly feel of Nick's hard body pressing atop her.

His hands - his glorious, skilled, wonderful hands – moved up and down the length of her body, removing clothing, stroking, squeezing, caressing. His mouth, too, was busy, trailing behind his hands, doing the most wonderful things. Open-mouthed kisses, eye-crossing swirls of his tongue, and stinging nips of sharp teeth soon had her writhing beneath him.

Isobeille thought she knew what it was like to feel desire for a man, but she was so very wrong. Nothing came close to the powerful waves crashing into her now, threatening to turn her mind into mush and the rest of her into a molten puddle of want and need. Nick, with his ardent and thorough attention, had somehow transformed her entire body into one pulsing, throbbing, erogenous zone. She ached, inside and out; it was at once agonizing and exquisite.

As she lay there, reveling in these wondrous new sensations, there was some far-away voice in her head that suggested that she should be a more active participant as Nick worked his magic. In truth, there was little she could do. Without conscious thought, her hands were already grabbing blindly at his hair, his shoulders, his biceps, unable to do anything more than just *hold on* for dear life.

And then her hands gripped nothing but air as Nick positioned himself between her thighs. Feeling the loss of his weight and heat acutely, she lifted her head and began to protest. Her eyes widened when she realized where he was, what he was about to do. She had heard of such things before, mainly from the whores at the pub her father often frequented, but never had she imagined a man wanting to please her this way.

She blinked, certain she was hallucinating, but when she opened her eyes again, there he was, looking up at her with a wicked glint in his eye.

"Do you know how many times I've dreamed of tasting you, Isobeille?" he said, his voice rough and barely intelligible.

A small whimper sounded in the back of her throat, but it was unlikely he heard it. His attention was focused elsewhere. Both of his large hands pressed against the inside of her thighs, opening her to him, his eyes blazing with desire as he gazed upon a part of her no man had ever seen.

"Beautiful," he whispered. "Just fucking beautiful."

For one irrational moment, she thought about protesting, for surely no respectable lass would allow such a thing. Then he kissed her *there*, his full male lips soft and tender against her receptive flesh, and all rational thoughts fled her mind entirely, leaving her feeling light-headed and dizzy.

The initial pleasure was overwhelming, but it was nothing compared to what he did next. His tongue came out and flicked her in one particularly sensitive spot, causing her back to arch until naught but her feet and shoulders remained atop the bed.

He growled again and took instant and ruthless advantage of her vulnerable position. Wedging his shoulders beneath the backs of her thighs, he wrapped his powerful arms around her legs, angling her exactly where he wanted her.

Isobeille was soon lost in a world of sensation. A strange and wondrous pressure began to build as Nick feasted upon her, the sounds of his greedy pleasure feeding her own as he murmured and muttered against her. The words he spoke were raw and carnal, stripping away every sense of decency and propriety she had.

And then, just when she thought she could not possibly survive another second, the rapture seared through her like a bolt of lightning and she was no longer earthbound, but flying amidst the stars.

Nick slid up the length of her trembling body and pulled her into his arms. "Isobeille," he crooned softly as he placed gentle kisses at the corners of her lips. "My beautiful, sweet Isobeille. I want to spend the rest of my life making you feel just like this."

His voice travelled right into her soul, branding it as his lips had branded her body. For as long as she lived, it would be that voice that would always reach her, that voice that would command her heart. She was his, she had been from that very first moment on the sidewalk when she had looked into his eyes. He had given her so much. Now it was time for her to give him the only thing she could.

"Nick," she murmured once she was able to speak again, "I need ye."

"You have me, Isobeille." He petted her softly. She could feel the hard proof of his need, yet he made no move to join with her.

"Not all of ye."

His eyes flashed, filled with fire and heat and want and need, but he still held back. "We can wait. Until you're sure. Until you're ready."

She cupped his face with her hand. "I am sure. Verra sure. And verra ready."

His lips tilted a little at the corner. "You haven't said yes yet, Isobeille."

"Yer hearing must be failing, for I recall screaming that verra word quite loudly only a wee bit ago."

Nick chuckled and nuzzled the soft spot just behind her ear. "You know what I mean, Isobeille."

"I do ken it."

"Then say yes, Isobeille. Say you will marry me."

She looked into his eyes, staring into the soul of the man she loved more than anything on earth.

"Aye, Nick Peterson, I would be honored te be yer bride."

Nick took full and instant possession of her mouth. "I love you, Isobeille."

"And I ye," she said, fidgeting beneath him. "Can we be getting along with the claiming now?"

"Impatient, are we?" he laughed, but he was already positioning his body over hers. She hissed in pleasure at the feel of his skin, naked and hot against hers. She reached down between them and grasped him in her hand, guiding him to where she needed him most.

"Have I told ye ye are a bonnie, fine mon?"

He smirked and kissed the corners of her lips. "You have."

"Ah. I think we must be adding braw and large as weel."

His eyes shone with love as he brushed the hair away from her face. "You are sure about this, Isobeille? You don't want to wait?"

"Verra sure."

In case he needed further encouragement, she

slid her hands over his tight backside and angled her hips in invitation. His eyes never left hers as he began to push forward very slowly.

It was a wondrous thing, the sensation of him coming inside of her, entering her body for the first time. She held her breath as she stretched around him, adjusted to him. His mouth closed over hers, thrusting through her maidenhead until he was seated deeply inside her.

"Are you alright?" he whispered, holding himself still.

"Aye," she answered breathlessly. "Do please continue."

He laughed again and began moving slowly, stoking her desire until it threatened to set them both aflame. Only then did he increase his pace and the force of his thrusts. Isobeille instinctively lifted her hips to take him even deeper, wanting to wrap herself around him completely, to hold on tight and never let him go.

Before long the telltale tingle began to grip her once again as it built in intensity. Isobeille's nails curled into his back; Nick hissed and clenched his teeth as she tightened around him. Mouth opened in a silent scream, she shattered even as she felt the warmth exploding deep within.

"I love you, Isobeille," Nick whispered, placing one more kiss to her lips, this one infinitely tender.

She wrapped her arms around him and kissed him back, murmuring words that made his heart soar. "And 'tis a good thing ye do, Nick Peterson, for ye *will* be making an honest woman of me now."

Epilogue

Nick managed to finagle a couple of days off and took Isobeille home to meet his mother during the week between Christmas and New Year's. Since it was the holiday, most of Nick's brothers and sisters were visiting with their families, too. Isobeille was instantly adored, as he knew she would be. It scared him a little, actually, because there were times when his family seemed more interested in Isobeille than him, but he didn't mind too much, because he made sure he was always by Isobeille's side.

For her part, Isobeille blossomed under their attention. Nick had never seen her smile so much nor look quite so radiant. Of course, he liked to think that he had a lot to do with that, too.

When the new semester began in mid-January, Isobeille officially began her first real job as Ian's personal research assistant. She sat through his lectures, and helped him with his research. Her fluency with ancient languages was a tremendous asset, as was her knowledge of many things that had been lost to time.

Isobeille took to the academic life like a fish to

water. Her new position gave her carte blanche access to the University resources, and for a woman who was always too curious for her own good, it was nothing less than nirvana.

Ian's students loved her, and she, in turn, thrived under all of the positive attention. It was a bit overwhelming at first, but Ian was quite protective of her; he kept her under his watchful eye and ensured that he was always nearby, at least until she became more acclimated to her new world.

Nick loved seeing her happy, loved seeing the sparkle in her eye when she told him about whatever new fascinating thing she'd uncovered that day. They still had breakfast together and most nights, dinner, too, though sometimes it was Nick surprising Isobeille with a home-cooked meal (or take-out) when Ian had a late lecture (Mrs. Anderson was only too glad to help).

Ian turned out to be a valuable ally and friend, as well. True to his word, he helped Isobeille get all of her papers in order. It took some doing, and a couple more pieces of her dowry to the right people over in Scotland, but eventually Isobeille Aislinn McKenna had a legal birth certificate (they listed her birth year as 1990 instead of 1390).

Two days after the paperwork was finalized, Nick and Isobeille were married in a small, quiet ceremony. Only once he slipped that golden band onto her finger, did Nick finally breathe a sigh of relief. His greatest fear was that somehow Isobeille would be taken away before he could fully bind her to him. He didn't really believe that Fate would be so cruel, but then again, that knight back in Gwynnevael probably hadn't thought so, either.

Each night, Isobeille found the most amazing ways to reassure him that *he* was the real reason she had travelled six hundred years into the future.

There was no longer any doubt in his mind that Isobeille was his soul mate.

For all of eternity.

Glossary

afore	before
albeit	although
amnae	am not
aye	yes
behoove	to be necessary or proper for
cannae	can not
coffer	treasury, funds
dinnae	did not
doesna	does not
doona	do not
garderobe	a medieval bathroom
inte	into
isnae	is not
ken	know, understand, comprehend, perceive
laird	lord, overseer
mayhap	maybe, perhaps
mon	man
sennight	week
te	to
tome	book
trencher	plate
trews	close-fitting trousers
untoward	improper
verra	very
wee	small, little, tiny
wouldnae	would not
ye	you

Thanks for reading Isobeille's story

... but it's not the end. Remember Newton's Third Law: For every action, there is an equal and opposite reaction. If Isobeille came forward, then someone else has to go back.

If you want to see what happens when a modern-day NYC girl wakes up in 15th century Scotland, check out Aislinn's story in ***Raising Hell in the Highlands*** (formerly titled Lost in Time II) - keep reading for an excerpt

If you liked this book, then please consider posting a review online! It's really easy, only takes a few minutes, and makes a huge difference to independent authors who don't have the mega-budgets of the big-time publishers behind them.

Log on to your favorite online retailer (or Goodreads) and just tell others what you thought, even if it's just a line or two. That's it! A good review is one of the nicest things you can do for any author.

As always, I welcome feedback. Email me at abbiezandersromance@gmail.com. Or sign up for my mailing list on my website at http://www.abbiezandersromance.com for up to date info and advance notices on new releases, Like my FB page (AbbieZandersRomance), and/or follow me on Twitter (@AbbieZanders).

Thanks again, and may all of your ever-afters be happy ones!

♥ *Abbie*

Excerpt From *Raising Hell in the Highlands*

Aislinn slowly returned to consciousness. Her eyes were heavy, her limbs like lead. For all intents and purposes, it felt like she was suffering the aftereffects of one hell of a bender, though she was not one to overindulge. As a rule, Aislinn liked to remain in complete control of her faculties, and would never willingly have made herself that vulnerable, especially not without her team to watch her six.

The errant thought slipped through the walls she'd erected around her heart and scored a direct hit before she could stop it.

You don't have a team anymore.

Before the survivor's guilt could gain full hold again, she forced those thoughts away, citing the mantra the Army shrink had made her repeat until she could almost believe it: There was nothing she could have done. Nothing anyone could have done. Bad shit happens.

So what the hell had happened this time? She tried to think back. She remembered leaving the church, walking up and down the streets, her feet taking her where she needed to be. Usually it was the bus station, or a train station, or the occasional dock - someplace where the criminal element thrived. Somewhere where it wasn't difficult to find someone who could benefit from her taxpayer-funded skills training and life experiences.

But she hadn't been drawn to any of the usual haunts. After wandering aimlessly for a while, she had cleared her mind and found herself moving toward the park. She must have circled the outer path twice before coming upon the pile of shivering rags huddled between the bench and the trees.

It wasn't the first time, and the odds were that it wouldn't be the last. There were too many like that. Too many homeless, too many addicts, too many who had no place to go and no one they could turn to for help.

She remembered reaching down to see exactly what she was dealing with when she felt the back of her head explode and everything went black…

Aislinn lifted her hand and gingerly touched the base of her skull, wincing when it shot a fresh wave of pain right through to her frontal lobe. Her fingers came away sticky and dark, which meant the wound was probably still bleeding a little, but it didn't seem to be life-threatening at least. She'd had a lot worse.

Thank God for small favors, she thought wryly.

She'd definitely had her bell rung, though, as evidenced by her current level of disorientation. Aislinn endeavored to push the pain and haze into the background and focus. Distraction was a good way to get herself killed. Or worse.

She could feel the grass beneath her and see the fuzzy outline of trees through her blurred vision, but it felt different somehow. It was no longer dark, she realized; maybe that's what was throwing her off. Exactly how long had she been out?

Her hands automatically went toward her weapons as she patted around her body. *All present and accounted for*, she thought, sighing with relief. Even her pack was still loosely slung over one shoulder.

She pushed herself up to sitting, closing her eyes while the world spun wildly around her and messed with her senses.

It wasn't just the daylight that seemed incongruous. Aislinn didn't feel the biting cold as she should, either. Snow had already begun to fall in earnest during her last foray along the path, promising a white Christmas for the first time in years. But rather than finding herself face down on frozen ground, she was laying on what appeared to be soft – albeit uncut – grass. And it was *warm*.

The scents were all wrong, too. Snow had its own smell – anyone who spent any time up North knew that. But there was no hint of it now. Nor was there any discernable whiff of trash, dead leaves, or the ever-present aromas of stale beer and urine usually so prevalent in the park. She expanded her lungs, pleased when they didn't protest too much, and drew in the scents of grass, clean air, and oddly enough, something that smelled like dried herbs. Lavender, maybe, or heather.

Her senses were returning to her slowly but surely. As her hearing came back online and the annoying buzz faded, her brain struggled to identify the sounds. One was easy enough – men. Loud, bellowing men, grunting and spewing forth colorful vulgarities in a thick brogue.

And … horses? Not that she was particularly familiar with the beasts, but even she could recognize a few snorts and whinnies.

There was something else, too – a repeated, rhythmic clanging that resounded in her skull painfully and immediately roused her self-preservation instinct.

She rubbed at her eyes until the last of the little black dots faded away. And then shut them again quickly in disbelief. Clearly the blow to her head had caused significant damage, because there was no way what she had seen could be real. She decided she must be suffering from some kind of displaced psychosis resulting from a head injury and repeated viewings of *The Highlander* during late night bouts of insomnia.

She pinched herself – *hard* – then opened her eyes again, but the surreal scene hadn't faded. She tried again and caught her breath. *Yep. Still there.*

The more she watched – she had quite a vivid subconscious imagination, it seemed – the more entranced she became. Especially by the supersized guy sporting the black and green plaid. A warrior, for sure, with his long, flowing auburn hair braided at the temples and a symphony of rippling muscles. With the face of an archangel – hard and masculine yet otherworldly beautiful, sinfully defined arms and legs, he moved with lethal grace and skill.

Despite his size and obvious proficiency in combat, he seemed to be a bit overwhelmed at that moment. Aislinn counted no less than six men attacking the warrior all at once. They, too, were large men sporting kilts, but they didn't have the same skill with a sword – *and holy shit, was that an axe?* - as the really big one, and the colors of their plaids were different.

The big guy was holding his own, she noted with no little amount of respect. But then a movement in her peripheral vision caught her attention. As Aislinn watched in growing horror, three more men emerged from the trees behind the warrior. With all of his focus on those in front of him and along his sides, he didn't see the threat as she did.

It's just a dream, she told herself, most likely the result of blunt-force head trauma. But before she could fully process that thought, she was on her feet, shoving her personal discomfort aside and stealthily moving toward the action as her training kicked in. It might be just a dream, but it was *her* dream, and she'd be damned if she'd allow such a fine warrior to go down by a sword to the back in any dream of hers.

Aislinn launched herself into the fray, pulling her blades from her boots as she did so. In a series of lightning fast kicks and spins, she took out the three men attacking her warrior from behind before they even knew what hit them. As the Mel Gibson look-alike turned around to see the commotion, she caught the flash of a sword sailing through the air – right at her warrior's head.

Also by Abbie Zanders

Contemporary Romance

- Dangerous Secrets (Callaghan Brothers #1)
- First and Only (Callaghan Brothers #2)
- House Calls (Callaghan Brothers #3)
- Seeking Vengeance (Callaghan Brothers #4)
- Guardian Angel (Callaghan Brothers #5)
- Beyond Affection (Callaghan Brothers #6)
- Having Faith (Callaghan Brothers #7)
- Bottom Line (Callaghan Brothers #8)
- Callaghan Brothers Guide (series companion)
- Five Minute Man (Covendale Series #1)
- All Night Woman (Covendale Series #2)
- The Realist
- Celestial Desire
- Celina (Connelly Cousins, Book #1)
- Johnny (Connelly Cousins, Book #2)

Time Travel Romance

- Raising Hell in the Highlands (A Timeless Love, Book #2; formerly Lost in Time II)

Paranormal

- Vampire, Unaware

- Black Wolfe's Mate (writing as Avelyn McCrae)

About the Author

Abbie Zanders loves to read and write romance in all forms; she is quite obsessive, really. Her ultimate fantasy is to spend all of her free time doing both, preferably in a secluded mountain cabin overlooking a pristine lake, though a private beach on a lush tropical island works, too. Sharing her work with others of similar mind is a dream come true. She promises her readers two things: no cliffhangers, and there will always be a happy ending. Beyond that, you never know…

Made in the USA
Middletown, DE
16 May 2016